Love and Betrayal

By: CoCo J.

Published by Sullivan Productions LLC
www.leolsullivan.com

Acknowledgments

*First off I would like too give a special thanks to the creator. Second my parents Kristie Fluker and Corey Hopson, who raised me to have respect and morals. My grandma's and great grandma's Linda Fluker-Garrison, Linda Garrison, and Nellie Fluker. My paw-paws Clifford Hopson Sr., and Donald Jump Pierre. My aunts Carolyn Whatley, Letha Fluker-Gill, Oretha Fluker, Sheila Agnew and Sabrina Hopson. My uncles Wayne Fluker, Victor Howard Jr., Clifford Jr., Derrick, and Karl Hopson. My two nannies, Marva Gibson and Lanelle Whatley. My siblings Lyneisha, Logan, Jayla, Corey, and Maya Fluker, my god sister and Brother La'Jara and Ja'Marcus Whatley. My two favorite girl cousins Kenya and Tylisha Fluker. My favorite boy cousins Labrian (Wussy) Fluker, and Desmond Whatley. My other cousins, Howard, Keith, Lafabian, Michael, Kenshawn Fluker, Chavez, Charles, Kendrick, Hopson, Derrick and Darrin Ellis, Anthony and Antonio Agnew, Deshawn, Chan and Anthony Hines. My girl cousins Latina, LaDonna, JayMalisa Whatley. Crystal, Jasmine, Santanna, and Sierra Fluker. Nyga, Keanna and Fantasia Hines. Daijonia Hopson and Tamia Agnew. My favorite Guy (Terry), my bestfriend Kiana Hall. Destiny Lockhart, Davon Jackson, Ta'Liyah Johnson, Mercedes Winters. Mita Rhodes (Your like an aunt too me lol) I love you all and thank y'all for always being there for me. *And if I forgot about you, SORRY!*

This books is dedicated too all my fallen angels.- *My paw-paw Wilmar (Chank) Garrison Jr., my great paw-paw Logan Fluker Sr. my Uncles Logan Jr, Steven (You know I'm always bout it bout it), Desmond, Keyshawn, Brandon Fluker. James Whatley, Lionel Garrison Sr. (My Parian) and my aunties. Donna Hines, Bernice Barconey, Frances Jemison. And my great-great grandma Madea. I love and miss you all. Continue too watch over me.*

A special thanks too Leo Sullivan, thank you for believing in me and letting me be apart of your team.

Je'leese

"This nigga must really think that just because it's about to be summer he can take me for a fucking fool and start acting crazy." I said to my best friends Katherine and Daivon as we sat in the kitchen in the apartment we shared in Taylor, Michigan.

"Girl, I don't even know why you trip over him. You know he's coming home to you." Daivon said.

"That's not the damn point Daivon. This nigga is going around the city with other bitches like they his girls while other people calling my phone trying to gossip about it. Do you think I want to hear that shit, especially while I'm sick?" I said irritated. I've been sick since the end of April and my man had people blowing up my phone telling me what he was doing out there with other bitches, and the shit Daivon was saying right now was really pissing me off. She's so lucky she's my best friend, because if she was just another female I would have been snapped on her ass.

"Leese, you don't know what happened. Just wait until he calls you and ask him about it." Katherine said. She was always trying to be the peacemaker when it came to me and my man Giovanni. I guess she knew how much I love him. But she was making me mad right now, too.

"Katt, you know me better than that." I said as I dialed Giovanni's number for the tenth time. This time somebody answered the phone. And it wasn't Giovanni.

"Hello." A female said.

"Who is this?" I asked not believing my damn ears.

"Who the fuck is this?" The female asked me.

"You answering Giovanni's phone so you should already know who I am. Now who the fuck is this?" I asked her getting madder and madder by the second.

"Don't fucking worry about it bitch! Just know your nigga is done with you hoe!" The female said.

"Oh yea, where are y'all at right now?" I asked her.

"We're in Flat Rock." She said.

"Okay, cool." I said hanging up the phone. I walked into the living room to get my purse and car keys. I made sure my baby 9mm was in there before I walked out the door.

"Where is yo crazy ass going?" Katt asked me.

"Giovanni's house. He got me fucked up for real this time," I said as I walked toward my car. My girls followed me.

"Aw shit." Daivon said as she locked the house up before running to my car.

"Man, I'm so tired of his shit I mean I love him to fucking death. But I'm not about to let him keep messing over me." I said as Katt got in the passenger side and Dai got in the back of my black Cadillac. As soon as the doors were closed I pulled off and drove to Giovanni's house, it was about a twenty minute drive from my apartment. But, the way I was driving, we made it there between ten and fifteen minutes.

When we got to Giovanni's house a Red Honda Accord was parked in Giovanni's drive way. I knew the Accord wasn't one of Giovanni's many cars, nor did it belong to his home boy Chris. I got out the car and left it running. I walked up to the door and knocked twice before I banged on it.

"Leese, what the hell are you doing here?" Giovanni asked me as he opened the door.

"Where that bitch at that answered your phone talking slick?" I asked him without raising my voice. I didn't see a point in having a screaming match with Giovanni. I just wanted that bitch to come out the house.

“Leesy man, please don’t do this shit.” Giovanni said.

“Naw, fuck that! The bitch wanted to talk slick, and I’m gone show her ass she fucking with the wrong one.” I said as I tried to get past him.

“Leese, man, just go home. I’ll be over there later.” He said.

“Tell that bitch to come outside, then I’ll go home.” I said.

“Katt, please come get ya girl.” Giovanni said. Katt just looked at him as the bitch who answered the phone walked up behind Giovanni.

“Bitch, you don’t want me to come out there.” The bitch said.

“Jasmine, go sit down man. I’m telling you this now and it’s for your own safety.” Giovanni said over his shoulder. But the bitch didn’t take his advice. She still came closer to the door talking shit. Once she was within my reach I grabbed her by her hair and pulled her past Giovanni. I let the bitch stand straight up so she could have a fair chance to fight me. But just by the look on her face, I knew the bitch was scary and wasn’t about that life. I started swinging on her. I hadn’t fought a bitch in about four months. I also had a lot of anger and pent up frustration, and I just took all that shit out on her. Hell, she deserved it for talking so much shit over the phone.

"Ahh, get this crazy bitch off me!" The bitch named Jasmine screamed as I was still hitting her. She was swinging her arms so wildly trying to hit me that she did hit me, right in my eye. That shit made me see red. I let her hair go and grabbed her around her neck and tried to choke the hell out of her.

"Bitch, talk that shit now." I said trying to choke the life out of her. Katt, Daivon, and Gee all ran up to me and tried to get my hands from around her neck.

"Leese, you're going to kill the girl." Katt said as they struggled harder to get my hands free. Once they finally got my hands free from around her neck she fell to the ground breathing hard trying to catch her breath. She had a black eye, a busted lip, and a bloody nose. I just laughed as Giovanni pulled me away from Katt, Dai, and Jasmine.

"What the fuck is wrong with you? You want these people out here to call the police?" He asked me once we were out of ear shot from the others.

"No, what the fuck is wrong with you nigga? I give you my all and you go around town with some bitch, then the bitch answered yo phone? Nigga you know you playing it too crazy, and fuck them people and the police. You know I don't give a fuck." I said.

"Man calm yo ass down. It wasn't even like that, I was on Linwood and Fenkell and Jasmine called me and said her car wouldn't start and she needed a jump. She was at a gas station calling me so I told her I would come get her, I picked her up and brought her to her car." Giovanni said.

"So now you playing 'Captain Save a Hoe'? You know what, don't even answer that question. I'm good on you." I said walking away from him.

"What the fuck you mean you good on me?" He asked me as he grabbed my arm and spun me around to face him.

"You heard what I said. I'm good on you. Find another female that's gone let you play with her feelings, because I'm truly done. So do you my mans." I said with tears in my eyes, but I refused to let them fall. I was done crying over his ass.

"Naw, you not done. Don't fucking play with me Je'leese." He said, and I knew he was mad just by the look in his eyes.

"We gone see." I said walking away from him.

"I'll be over there later. You better answer the damn door." He yelled as I walked back towards my car.

"Are you going to answer the door?" Dai asked me as we got in the car.

"Nope. I'm getting a room. I don't have time for him right now." I said as I pulled off. I didn't even see Jasmine. Her rat ass probably went back in the house.

"Well, you know we're going to be here for you. We might as well spend the night at the room too, because that nigga gone know when somebody is in the house." Katt said.

"I'll get y'all a room too." I said as the tears finally fell. My body was aching and I needed a bubble bath. I couldn't wait until I got to the hotel.

Giovanni

"How you gone let that bitch put her hands on me like that?" Jasmine asked me when she was done cleaning the blood off her face.

"Aye man, watch yo fucking mouth." I said as I sat on the sofa and turned on the television, which was on BET.

"Nigga, fuck that bitch! She put her hands on the wrong one." Jasmine said.

"Jasmine, you better chill the fuck out. You did that to yourself. Yo ass answered my phone trying to get some shit started and Je'leese finished it." I said laughing.

"And you gone take up for her?" She asked me. That was a stupid ass question to ask.

"What the fuck you think? That's my girl. Yo ass was in the wrong, not her." I said.

"That's yo girl, but you out here fucking around on her with me, and plenty more bitches." Jasmine said.

"No matter how many bitches I fuck with, she's the one I'll always want to be with, and the one I'll always be with. I tell all y'all hoes that from the jump. Now it's either you play yo role or get the fuck on. Matter of fact, get yo hoe ass out my house." I said.

"I got yo hoe." Jasmine said as she walked towards the door with her purse in her hand. "And tell that bitch to watch her back." She said as she walked out the front door. I didn't even say shit. I knew Je'leese could handle her own when it came down to fighting or whatever else them bitches would try. The only thing I was really worried about was her going to jail for trying to kill a hoe like Jasmine that would try to hop on tip with her or check her.

Je'leese's attitude was one of the many reasons I fell in love with her when she was just thirteen and I was fifteen. She was just like a fire cracker, once you lit a fire with her you'd better be ready for that big "BOOM" that came afterward. She was also a female version of me. She was five feet even with a brown skin complexion that went well with her hazel brown eyes. She didn't take shit from anyone, male or female. She would hop on tip quick as hell when it came to me and fucking around on her. Honestly, I don't know why I kept playing with her feelings, I knew if I pushed her to her limit she would shoot me and the bitch I'm fucking with.

I sat in my house giving Je'leese some time to cool down before I went over to the apartment she shared with her girls. I knew Katt would answer the door for me, but that bitch Daivon, she was sneaky as hell. I'd told Je'leese plenty of times about hanging with her, but she didn't listen to me. I was about to get up and get me a water when my phone rang. I didn't recognize the number.

"Hello?" I answered getting up.

"When am I going to see you again?" I heard Daivon ask from the other end of the phone.

"Bitch, why the hell are you calling me? Where is Je'leese?" I asked her.

"Calm yourself down, she and Katt just dropped me off at home." She giggled.

"What the fuck you want? You just saw what Je'leese did too Jasmine." I said walking into the kitchen.

"I'm not worried about that bitch." Daivon said.

"Watch yo fucking mouth hoe." I said as I looked through the fridge for a bottle of water.

"So, now I'm a hoe?" She asked.

"You been a hoe, that's nothing new. Why are you calling me? And what the fuck do you want?" I asked her, I was tired of this hoe. And I also knew by messing with her I could lose my life considering that she was Je'leese friend, well supposed to be friend.

"I wasn't a hoe when you fucked me, was I?" She asked.

"Bitch, you fucked me and Chris on the same night. That was a fucking train. And besides both me and Chris was drunk and didn't know what the fuck happened until the night after. But yeah you were a hoe then, and you're a hoe now. See that's what y'all hoes don't understand a nigga will make love to his woman but he'll fuck a hoe." I said laughing.

"What about the second time you fucked me?" She asked me.

"Bitch you know I was drunk on that night too." I said laughing again.

"Keep thinking you're funny and we're going to see how funny it is when Leese finds out you fucked her friend, not once, but twice." Daivon said as she let out an evil laugh.

"Bitch, don't fucking play with me. Both of them times was a mistake." I said through gritted teeth.

"Okay, whatever you say. You know Leese won't see it like that. She'll see it as a betrayal from both of us. And we both know I don't give a fuck about her feelings. You do." She said.

"Look bitch, I don't have time to play with you. What the hell do you want?" I asked her not trying to play any of her games.

"I want too fuck you tonight." She said.

“Bitch, yo ass must really be crazy.” I said.

“Nope, but Je’leese will be when I tell her that I’ve fucked her nigga not once, but twice.” She said.

“You no good dirty bitch.” I said.

“Call me what you want, but I bet she find out about us tonight, and I just might tell Katt that I fucked her nigga too.” She said.

“Where do you want to meet?” I asked her, I didn’t have time for her to be running her mouth to Katt and especially not Je’leese. I wanted to be the one to tell her.

“I’ll text you later with the details.” She said as she hung up the phone.

“Fuck!” I yelled as I put the phone down on the counter. I really wanted to kill this bitch.

Jasmine

"I can't believe this bitch put her fucking hands on me." I thought to myself. After I left Gee's house I went home, put some ice on my face and called my girl Dora. She came right over along with her ugly ass cousin Ashley.

"What the hell happened to your face?" Dora asked me, as Ashley laughed.

"Gee's bitch snuck me." I lied.

"How the hell did she know you was over there?" Dora asked me.

"I don't know. I guess she was trying to see him or some shit." I lied again.

"Man, I need to hurry up and let him know this news." Dora said.

"I'm mad as hell that bitch put her hands on me for nothing." I said.

"Don't worry about her, she won't be in the picture for much longer. As soon as Gee finds out he got me pregnant he's going to leave her ass for me." Dora said smiling, I didn't say anything. And I wasn't going to say anything. I knew Dora's baby wasn't by Gee; she was just trying to trap him. But her plan wasn't going to go through if I had anything to do with it.

It was four years ago when Dora, and I met Gee in club Climax. I was attracted to him from the first time I saw him. I didn't tell Dora that I wanted him, but later that night I kicked myself in the ass for not telling her. Because as we were leaving the club Dora and Gee exchanged numbers. I tried to be a good friend and stay away from him, but it seemed as if everywhere I went Gee was there also. One day while I was shopping at Somerset, he walked up to me and asked me for my number. That same night he hit me off with some money and some dick. Ever since then we've been fucking around. And I now know why this bitch Dora is so obsessed with him. He had the best dick in the city of Detroit. Not to mention the nigga was paid. Today Dora called me and asked me to pretend my car wouldn't start and I needed a jump. I called Gee to see if he could give me a jump. Of course he came. After that I followed him to his house saying I had to talk to him about something. Once I got there I was supposed to call Dora, but that silly shit right there was something I wasn't going to do. The only reason I went along with the plan was so I could get some money and some dick out of him. But when his bitch called and I answered the phone talking shit, I didn't think the hoe was gone come so that fucked up my plan, and I was mad as hell.

"Jasmine, do you hear me talking to you?" Dora asked me snapping me out of my thoughts.

"Huh? What did you say?" I asked her.

"I said do you want to try again tomorrow?" She asked me.

"I don't know, his bitch might be over there tomorrow." I said. I didn't want another confrontation with her crazy ass.

"Okay, we'll give it a few days." Dora said taking a sip of the apple juice she brought with her. I sat there looking at Dora with nothing but hatred in my eyes. I really did hate this bitch.

"Dora, are you ready to go?" Ashley asked her cousin, while giving me the evil eye.

"Why Ashley? We just got over here and now you want to leave." Dora said.

"Dora, don't play stupid. You know I don't like this dizzy hoe, and you got me all up in this bitch crib." Ashley said not taking her eyes off me letting me know she meant every word she was saying. This hoe had more balls than I thought she had.

"Ash I told you Jas is cool. And besides you and Asia, she's the only female that I can trust." Dora said. Was this bitch stupid? I thought to myself.

"Girl, stop playing yourself. This hoe is not your friend, and it looks like you're going to learn the hard way. I'll be waiting in the car because I refuse to stay in the presence of this hoe any longer." Ashley said as she finally took her eyes off me and looked at her cousin before walking out my front door.

"I'm sorry Jass, she just doesn't trust people." Dora said.

"It's cool. She don't have to trust me." I said not giving a fuck if the bitch trusted me or not.

"But I should go before her ass leave me here. I'll call you later." Dora said as she got up.

"Okay, you do that." I said as I walked over to the door. Once she was out the door, I watched her walk to the car before I closed and locked my door. Then I walked into my room and grabbed the 1800 bottle that had a few shots left in it. I promised myself I wasn't going to drink during the day anymore, but hell I needed it. I had a headache, and I needed to think of a master plan.

Katherine

I was sitting in the room at Greektown hotel waiting on my fiancé and the father of my son, Chris, to call me back. He and our son Chris Jr. were on their annual father and son fishing trip along with Chris' father Charles. But they were on their way back. I turned off the TV just as my phone rang.

"Hello?" I said.

"Wassup baby?" Chris asked.

"Nothing, how was everything?" I asked him.

"Everything was fine. I just can't wait to get home to my woman." He said.

"You know I can't wait until you get home either." I replied smiling.

"Lil Chris wants to speak to his mommy."

"Okay, put him on."

"Mommy?" I heard my seven year old son say.

"Yes baby?"

"I'm having fun with daddy and papa, but I wish you was here." Lil Chris said. He was a straight up momma's boy.

"I know baby boy, but you know when you go fishing that's just for you, your daddy, and papa. But when you come home I'll take you to the zoo or somewhere fun, how does that sound?" I asked him.

"It sounds fun, is daddy going to come?"

"Of course he is, why wouldn't he?" I asked laughing.

"I don't know mommy, but I'm about to give daddy back the phone. I'm sleepy."

"Okay baby boy, I love you."

"I love you more mommy." Lil Chris said as his daddy took the phone back.

"Pops said hey Miss Katherine." Chris announced.

"Tell him I said hello, and I'll be to see him and Mama Renee soon." I said as I listened to Chris deliver the message to his father.

"He said okay."

"Where are y'all at now?" I asked him.

"On our way back, we have like three more hours. Where are you at?"

"Greektown." I said as I lay back on the bed.

"What are you doing at Greektown?" He asked me with a slight rise in his tone.

"Leese and Gee got into it again. Some bitch answered his phone, we went over there and Leese fought the girl." I said laughing.

"Aw man, did she beat the girl ass?" Chris asked knowing how Je'leese's attitude was.

"You know she did. The girl was no competition for Leese. She tried to kill the poor girl. Me, Dai and Gee had to stop her from choking the girl to death." I said as I laughed.

"Man, that nigga Gee ain't gone learn. He my mans, but he keeps fucking around on Leese and she gone kill his ass for real."

"I know, I just hope he learn his lesson before my best friend go to jail for murder."

"Baby, I miss you." Chris said changing the subject.

"I miss you more my love. I think we should work on finding us a bigger house when you get home."

"Why? You pregnant or something?" He asked me.

“No I’m not pregnant Christopher. But I do want to have another baby before Lil Chris hits ten.” I said.

“Come on baby, you know the kind of life I live.” Chris said.

“Yeah, I know that Chris. You were living the same life when Lil Chris was born. What’s the difference between then and now?” I asked him.

“There is no difference baby, but you’re going to school and working at the store twenty four seven. I don’t think that would be fair to you.” He said.

“Chris, don’t give me that bullshit ass story. I was working and going to school when I got pregnant with Lil Chris. But we’ll talk more on the subject when you get home. Leese and I are having dinner and I need to get going.”

“Okay baby, I love you.”

“I love you more, and kiss Lil Chris for me.”

“Okay.” He said as we hung up the phone. Once we were off the phone I thought about the reasons Christopher didn’t want to have another baby. I mean when I was pregnant with Lil Chris I was working at Greenfield Plaza and I was also going to community college. Now, I want to get pregnant again but I’m still working at Greenfield Plaza and I just got done with my last semester of college. I got off the bed and walked over to where my bags were. I pulled out my flip flops because I didn't feel like wearing gym shoes anymore today.

Daivon

I knew I was wrong for fucking with Je'leese and Katherine's men yeah they both called me their friend. But I never claimed those bitches as my friends. I don't have any friends. I can say at one point in time they were my friends. But now I hate both of them hoes. I've known Je'leese and Katherine since I was eight, Je'leese was nine and Katherine was ten. The reason I hated Je'leese was simple. She had everything I always wanted as a kid. She was a spoiled little bitch and got everything she wanted from her parents, grandparents, and even from my parents and grandparents. I resented her parents because they had the type of relationship I wished my mom and dad had. My parents never loved each other. In fact, they hated each other guts and the only reason they use to put up with each other was because of me and the love they had for me. I was twelve when they finally called it quits, I was mad at my father because he actually left me and my mother. When I asked him why he wanted to leave my mother, he always gave me some bullshit ass story saying there wasn't any more love between them. But from what I could tell there was never any love between them. Later that year I asked my mother what was the reason and she told me.

"Honey, your father was cheating on me with a white woman. I told him I didn't want anything to do with him and to get out my house." My mother said as tears fell down her face.

"How did you know he was cheating?" I asked her.

"Because, the woman called the house phone asking to speak to your father. She said it was about their daughter they had together." My mother said.

I wiped the tears that fell down her eyes but they kept coming. Watching my mother cry made me cry. I felt heartbroken. Two weeks after he moved out the house with me and my mother, he moved in with his mistress. Two months later, they were married. That drove my mother insane. On my thirteenth birthday, my father showed up to my party with his wife and their daughter. And on that day my mother shot herself in front of my face. That was the same day I started hating my father, his wife, Je'leese, and her parents.

Two years after my mother killed herself Je'leese's parents died in a car crash. Je'leese's grandparents moved into the house that was owned by her mother and father. She begged them to let me move in with them. They said yes, and it was my choice. It was between my father and his new family or Je'leese and her grandparents. I chose to stay with Je'leese and her grandparents. Katherine was always around, and that was the reason I started hating that bitch. She had her head stuck so far up Je'leese's ass that she didn't really consider me as a best friend until Je'leese said she wanted both of her best friends to be best friends so we could all be best friends together. And even then, Katherine never really paid me attention. She didn't invite me to none of her sleepovers unless Je'leese said something about it.

I was sitting in my room at Greektown listening to music. I was in one of my zones thinking about all the things I was going to do to Gee when he got there. I was so caught up in my thoughts that I almost didn't hear somebody knocking on the door.

"Who is it?" I asked.

"It's us." Katt said from the other side of the door.

"Fuck! What do these bitches want now?" I said as I got off the bed and answered the door. "What's up?" I asked them.

"We're going to get something to eat, do you want to come?" Leese asked me.

"Naw, my friend is going to bring me something." I lied.

"What friend?" Katt asked me.

"You don't know him." I snapped. What the fuck was this bitch asking me questions for?

"Well, have fun boo." Leese said.

"Don't worry, I will." I said smirking as I closed the door. I didn't even wait until they walked away from the door. I wanted those bitches out my face. I walked back to the bed and sat back down. I was about to finish my thoughts about Giovanni's sexy ass.

Giovanni

I drove by Leese apartment, her car wasn't there and all the damn lights were off. So I called Katt's cell phone, twice. The first time it went to voicemail, and the second time she answered.

"Hello?"

"Where ya girl at?" I asked her.

"At the restaurant in the hotel with Leese." She said letting me know she was with her.

"What hotel?"

"Greektown." She replied

"What room?"

"Leese, what's your room number?" She asked Leese.

"710, why?" Je'leese asked.

"Because I forgot my room number, and I knew your room came before mine." Katt lied. "I'm room 712." She said to me.

"Good looking, Katt." I said.

"Don't fuck shit up." Katt said, and I knew she was telling me not to fuck up again.

"I got you." I said hanging up the phone. I liked Katt; she was like a little sister to me. She had my back no matter what. I was on my way home from checking on my shops when my mans Chris called me.

"Hello?" I answered.

"Yo, what's the word?" He asked me.

"Ain't shit. Man you know how it is daily." I said.

"I heard Leese had to act a fool today." He said laughing.

"Yeah man, that dizzy hoe Jasmine answered my phone and was talking slick to Leese, she came over to the house and gave ole girl the hands and tried to choke her. I'm just glad she ain't go to her car. You know Leesy always have her baby with her." I said letting him know that Leese always carried her baby 9mm around.

"You ain't gone be happy until she kills you huh?" Chris asked.

"I just said the same thing after she left. But Je'leese loves me too much to kill me."

"Yeah aight, man you keep playing with her feelings and she gone kill you."

"When are you going to tell Katt about Christina?" I asked him about his daughter outside of his relationship with Katt.

"I don't know man, but she keeps pressuring me about having another baby. Then I got this bitch Ashley talking hella shit. She's trying to take all my damn money because I'm keeping Christina a secret." He said.

"Man these hoes crazy as hell." I said as I pulled into my driveway and saw Dora sitting on my porch.

"Man, tell me about it." He said as I turned my car off.

"Look, let me hit you back in a few. This bitch Dora sitting on my porch."

"Aight man." Chris said as we both hung up the phone.

"What the hell does this bitch want now?" I asked myself aloud.

"Hey." She said, I looked at her face, and it looked as if she had been crying.

"Wassup? What are you doing over here?" I asked her.

"We need to talk." She said.

"Then you need to make it snappy. I got some shit to do." I said as I opened the house door.

"I'm pregnant." She blurted out. I stopped in my tracks as I was walking in the living room. I knew for a fact that the only female I'd ever fucked without a condom was Je'leese. So if she was trying to say I was the father of her child she'd better get the fuck on.

"What you telling me for? It ain't mine." I said as I turned around to face her.

"What do you mean it ain't yours? Who else's would it be?" She asked putting her hands on her hips.

"It belong to one of them other niggas you fucking. I know I'm not the only nigga you out here fucking, so don't try and act like I am." I said.

"I haven't been fucking anybody else but you Gee! This baby is yours!" She yelled as she let the tears fall down her face, but those damn tears weren't fazing me.

"Bitch we both know that baby don't belong to me. I used a condom every time I ran up in yo nasty ass." I said.

"So, what you trying to say?" She asked me with a dumb look on her face.

"Bitch I know you not dumb and I also know yo ass can understand English. Now get the fuck on and stop wasting my time." I said as I grabbed the little velvet box from the entertainment center and walked towards the door.

"Okay cool, we're going to see when this baby gets here." She said as she walked out the door and walked to her car. I wasn't worried about shit she was saying because I knew for a fact her baby wasn't mine.

Chris

I was getting on the freeway from dropping my pops off at his house and on my way to my house when my cell phone rang. I looked at the screen and it was my second baby mama, Ashley.

"Hello." I said as I turned the music up just a little bit. I didn't want Lil Chris to wake up and hear anything.

"Where are you?" She asked me.

"Bitch, don't fucking call my phone questioning me. You know better than that." I said.

"Calm down, are you going to come see me tonight." She asked.

"I got my son." I said.

"What's your point? I got your fucking daughter, who wants to see you." She said.

"Ashley, I just got back in town. Let me settle back in then I'll come see her, damn."

"Fuck you Chris! I bet yo bitch know about Christina when I send her these pictures."

"Ashley, don't fucking play with me." I said through gritted teeth.

"Bye nigga." She said as she hung up the phone on me.

"Man fuck!" I screamed hitting the steering wheel.

"What's wrong daddy?" Lil Chris asked me from the back seat.

"Nothing son." I said as I turned the music down.

"Are we going to see mommy?" He asked me.

"We can, but she's probably sleep."

"So, she's going to wake up for me." He said.

"Okay son." I said smiling.

When we got to Greektown I told the woman that was working the front desk that I was married to Katherine, and that I needed to talk to her about our son who I had in my arms. Lil Chris was wide awake and ready to see his mother.

"Okay sir, just don't tell anyone I gave you the key." She said as she handed me the key card. Lil Chris and I got on the elevator and got off on the seventh floor, we walked until we stood in front of Katherine's room.

"Are you ready for this?" I asked Lil Chris.

"Yes sir." He said. I put him down and opened the door. As soon as the door was fully opened Lil Chris ran in and jumped on the bed.

"Mommy, mommy, wake up!" He yelled as he shook her.

"Huh, what's going on?" She asked as she sat up. She smiled once she saw me standing there and Lil Chris sitting on the bed. "When did y'all get here?"

"Just now, he wanted to see his mommy." I said smiling as I walked over to the bed. After she gave Lil Chris a kiss, she kissed me.

"I miss y'all." She said.

"We miss you too baby." I said as her phone beeped.

"Chris, can you hand me my phone?" She asked.

"Nah baby, you see I don't have my cell phone out right now. You can't have yours out." I said smiling.

"But it might be Leese." She said.

"Baby, I'm sure Leese is next door sleeping. If it was her and it was important she would have came and knocked on the door." I said.

"You're right." She said as she turned her attention to Lil Chris. I knew that it was Ashley with them pictures. I was just glad Katherine didn’t have a password on her phone like most females. When she went to sleep I was going to delete them pictures. I didn’t need her to find out about Christina. At least not right now.

Giovanni

When I got to Greektown I texted Katt and asked her where Leese was at.

"She's in her room, and the next time you fuck up I will not, and I mean WILL NOT help you ever again. She's my best friend and I'm tired of seeing her get hurt by you. And I also don't need her going to jail for killing you or one of your many hoes." Katt texted back.

"I got you Katt man, today wasn't even how she think it was. But I'll tell you about it later." I texted back, then got out my car and headed towards the front door of the hotel. I had Katt leave a key for Leese's room at the front desk. She told the woman that was working there that I would be coming to pick it up. I got the key from the front desk, and hopped on the elevator. I got off on the seventh floor, when I made it to Leese's room I stood out there for a minute before I put the key in the door and opened it.

"Katt, is that you?" Leese asked from the bathroom. I didn't answer her; I just went sat on the bed and waited until she walked out the bathroom. When she did walk out the bathroom, her hair was wet and curly and she had a towel wrapped around her. That gave my dick a sudden rise. But when I looked into her eyes she was looking like she wanted to kill me. "What are you doing here? And how did you get in my room?" She asked me.

"Katt left me the room key at the front desk and I came to talk to you." I said as I walked closer to her.

"There's nothing to talk about. I told you at your house that I was done with you, and that's what I meant." She said as she put on the plush robe that was on the bed. Then she walked by the window and turned the air on.

"Leesy, listen to me. I promise you that I didn't fuck her today, nor was I going to. She followed me home after I gave her a jump. She said she had something to talk to me about. I let her come in and I went to use the bathroom. That's when you called, I didn't know what happened until you started banging on the door. She didn't tell me that she answered my phone until you was knocking on the door." I said.

"Giovanni, do I look like boo-boo the damn fool?" She asked.

"No Leesy, you do not look like boo-boo the fool. You know I'd never lie to you about nothing. Yeah, I fucked her before. But I promise you I didn't fuck her today and I wasn't going to." I said.

"Giovanni, I'm tired of all the bullshit you put me through. I just need a break from you." She said.

"Leese, you don't mean that because you know I love you and I don't want a break from you. In fact, I want you to be my wife, and the mother of my children." I said as I pulled out the Velvet box. "I just want you to know that I didn't just pull this out because you're mad at me. I pulled it out because I love you and need you in my life. You know my life wouldn't be complete if you wasn't in it. Will you marry me?" I asked her as the tears welled up in my eyes. I walked closer to her; she was staring at the ground. I placed the ring on her left hand then lifted her chin up so that I could kiss her.

"Can you please get away from me?" She asked as she tried to push me away. "I meant what I said, I really am done with you." she said.

"No you're not." I said as I pushed her all the way against the wall. I leaned down and tried to kiss her again, this time she gave in and kissed me back as she wrapped her arms around my neck. When she stuck her tongue in my mouth, my dick came to life. It was already ready just from seeing her in the towel. I quickly took off my Foams that I had on. The only time we broke our kiss was when Leese helped me take off my white t-shirt. I picked her up and she wrapped her legs around my waist. I carried her to the bed, and laid her on it. I untied the robe she had on then got back to kissing her. I went from her lips, to her neck, down to her chest, her belly button, then down to her thighs. From her thighs I went to her clit, and she was already in the zone. I knew she was about to reach her climax just by the way her legs clenched around my neck. She gripped the back of my head with her hands and I ate her until she came all over my face. Once she came, I got up and kissed her lips.

"You taste so good." I said after I broke the kiss to look into her eyes. I knew Je'leese was the only woman for me, but I just didn't know if I could stop cheating. It was something about running up in some pussy that didn't belong to me. But Je'leese had the best pussy, hands down. I thrust my dick inside of her and she gasped. Then she moaned out in pleasure as I stroked her. She dug her nails into my back as she moved her hips to match my strokes. She pulled me closer to her so I could go deeper causing her to scream out and moan louder than ever.

"Ooooh." She moaned. "Please, don't stop!" She yelled.

"Fuck Leesy!" I groaned.

"Mhm, you feel so good baby." She said as she closed her eyes and tilted her head back.

"I-I'm sorry, I really am." I said as I picked up the pace of my strokes.

"Oh, god I'm cuming." She moaned in pleasure as her whole body shook.

"I'm cuming too baby!" I said as I shut my eyes.

"Ahhhhhh!" She yelled as I felt her walls clench around my dick as she came, which caused me to cum right after her. I collapsed on top of her. We both were breathing heavily.

"I never meant to hurt you." I whispered as I planted kisses all over her neck and shoulders. "I'm sorry and I love you." I said looking at her face. Her eyes were closed. I was about to doze off right along with her until my phone beeped. It was a text message.

"I'm at Greektown. Room 714, you have twenty minutes to be here." Daivon said. I looked at the phone and couldn't believe this bitch had the nerves to text me saying she was at the same hotel as Je'leese.

"And what if I don't come?" I asked her.

"Then your precious Je'leese will get these!" She texted back, and she attached three photos of us fucking.

"Bitch, where the fuck you get them from?" I texted her.

"Don't worry about that. Either you be here or I'll send them to her." She said.

"Fuck!" I said aloud forgetting Je'leese was asleep next to me. She turned towards me and moved closer.

"Baby, I need to go handle something at one of the shops. I'll be back in a few." I said into her ear.

“Mhm.” She mumbled.

I kissed her forehead, got up, and put my clothes on.

Daivon

I was sitting on my bed fresh out the shower waiting on Gee to come. I knew when he got there he was going to tell me to delete the pictures I had of us, and that was the very reason I had two extra copies made. When I heard somebody knocking on the door I thought it was one of them irritating hoes Je'leese or Katherine. I rolled my eyes then looked into the peep hole. I was surprised when I saw Gee standing there with a sour look on his face. I opened the door smiling.

"Well, you got here fast." I said stepping aside so he could come in.

"Bitch I did not come here to play games with you, nor did I come here to have a conversation with you. And before I leave out this damn room I want them fucking pictures deleted." He said as he walked in.

"Okay, fine." I said smiling. He started to take his clothes off, and I took off the thong and matching bra I had on. Once both of us stood naked I walked over to him and tried to kiss him, but he stepped back.

"Bitch, I ain't about to kiss yo trifling ass." He said with venom in his voice.

"Why are you so damn rude?" I asked him.

"Daivon, don't fucking play with me right now." He said.

"Okay, okay." I said as I got down on my knees and put his eleven inches in my mouth. He tried to pretend he wasn't into it, but I knew he was. I smiled knowing that he wasn't going to stay hostile after I put my lips to work. I sucked on his dick and balls. I knew I was doing a good job because when I looked down his toes were curled.

"Damn!" He said as he grabbed the back of my head and started to fuck my face. "I'm about to cum." I wanted him to cum in my mouth, but he pushed my head away from him and shot his load on the ground.

"I swear, you taste so good." I said as I got on the bed.

"Yeah, whatever bitch." He said.

I was laying on my back waiting on him to enter me. He just stood there stroking his eleven inches. I smiled as he walked towards me. "Turn the fuck over." He said. I did as he said; as soon as I was on all four he entered me thrusting all of him inside of me.

"Ooh!" I moaned. He was pounding so fast that the shit was hurting, but it felt so good at the same time. I didn't want him to stop. I grabbed the sheets and tried to run, but he pulled me back. "Damn, this feels so good." I said. I was on the verge of cuming. My whole body was shaking, my eyes rolled in the back of my head, and it felt like my body was on fire. But before I came Gee pulled out. I turned around and looked at him and realized he had a condom on, and it was full of cum.

"When did you put that on?" I asked him.

"Don't worry about it." He said as he grabbed his pants and walked into the bathroom. He turned the shower on. I waited ten minutes before I got out the bed and walked into the bathroom. Gee was in the shower. I stepped in it with him and rubbed his back. He turned around and grabbed me around my neck choking the hell out of me to the point where I couldn't breathe.

"Bitch, let me tell yo trifling ass something, if you ever threaten me again I will kill you! And don't fucking call my phone again, don't ever text me. And I mean that shit!" He said as he got out shower, grabbed his clothes and walked out the bathroom.

Je'leese

I woke up around two in the morning thinking I was going to find Giovanni in the bed with me, but I was wrong. I guess some things would never change. I laid there looking at the engagement ring Giovanni placed on my finger just a few hours ago. I smiled thinking about becoming Mrs. Giovanni Robert Smith. I sat up grabbed the remote then turned the TV on that was in the room. I put it on BET; they were playing the movie 'Streets' starring Meek Mill. That was me and Giovanni's movie. I got out the bed, walked over to the mini fridge, grabbed me a bag of chips and a bottle of water, and then walked back over to the bed. As I lifted my feet to get back in the bed I had the urge to throw up. I dropped the bottle and the chips from my hand and ran to the bathroom. I was so glad I made it just in time. I was leaning over the toilet for like five minutes.

"Leesy?" Giovanni called out.

"I'm in the bathroom." I managed to say as I got up from the floor.

"Are you okay?" He asked me as he walked into the bathroom.

"No." I said as I walked over to the sink to wash my face and brush my teeth.

"What's wrong?" He asked me.

"I don't know. I just feel so weak right now." I said as I walked back into the room.

"Get back in the bed, do you want something to eat? I can call room service or go and get something." He said.

"No, I'm fine. I just want to lay down." I said as I got back into the bed, he took his shirt, pants, and basketball shorts off and got in the bed with me.

"I love you Je'leese." He said as he kissed my forehead.

"Where were you at?" I asked him.

"I had to handle some shit at one of the shops. Some lil nigga was fucking shit up." He said as he looked at me.

"Are you ever going to leave that shit alone?" I asked him.

"Soon baby, I promise you. I just need to tie up a few loose ends then I'm done and we can move away from Detroit." He said.

"Move where? I don't want to leave Katt or Dai." I said.

"Baby, Katt has a family, but luckily for y'all, me and Chris have been talking about moving to Cali, ATL, or Vegas. And fuck that bitch Daivon!" He said.

"Why don't you like Dai? What has she ever done to you?" I asked.

"Baby girl, Daivon is a fucking snake. And I wish you get that through your damn head and leave that hoe alone." He said.

"Giovanni, me, Katt and Dai have been friends since we were all kids. You know me and Katt aren't going to leave her." I said.

"Baby, Daivon is a grown woman. She don't need to be following you everywhere you go, especially if we're talking about starting a family." He said. I knew if we kept this conversation going it was going to end up in an argument, and that was something I didn't want to happen. I wasn't feeling good, my head was spinning. And I didn't have the strength to argue with him

"Whatever." Was all I said, and he knew I wasn't going to say anything more about it.

"Je'leese?" He called once my eyes were closed.

"Yes?" I answered him.

"Do you love me?" He asked me.

"Yes I love you." I said.

"No matter what I do, will you always love me?" He asked me. I opened my eyes and looked at him.

"Giovanni, yes I will always love you no matter what. You're my first and only love. Where is this coming from?" I said looking into his eyes.

"I'm glad to know that." He said kissing me on my forehead.

"Are the police after you or something?" I asked him.

"Leesy, you know I'm too good for the police to be after me. I just wanted to make sure I have my girl for life." He said as he smiled, which caused me to smile.

The next morning I woke up around ten. I was still feeling the same way I felt all day the previous day and the night before. I didn't know what was going on with me. I sat up in the bed and turned the TV off. My head was still spinning and the TV was making it worse.

"When did you get up?" Giovanni asked me as he walked out the bathroom with just a towel wrapped around his waist.

"I just got up." I told him staring at his body, which had water dripping down it.

"How are you feeling?" He asked smirking when he noticed I was staring at his body.

"Still the same." I said, he walked over to the bed and sat down.

"When do you check out?" He asked me.

"Twelve thirty." I said.

"Okay, when you leave here I'm taking you to my house." He said.

"Katt and Dai rode here with me, so how will they get home?" I asked him.

"Chris can take Katt home, that bitch Daivon can walk for all I care." He said as he got out the bed, walked over to the window, and looked out of it.

"Giovanni!" I said.

"What?" He asked turning to look at me.

"She's my friend." I said.

"No, she's a snake. But I'll see if Chris can take her home." He said.

*****

It was June 2nd and I hadn't seen my friends in two weeks. Katt called me yesterday morning and told me her and Lil Chris would be at the apartment today so she could get some clothes. And I needed to do the same thing. I was in my black on black Bentley that Giovanni bought me for my 21st birthday as I drove to the apartment. When I got there Katt and Dai were sitting in the living room while Lil Chris was playing on the floor.

"Hey Lil Chris." I said.

"Hey nanny." Lil Chris said as he got up off the floor and hugged me.

"Girl, we thought Gee wasn't going to let you come." Daivon said.

"Giovanni doesn't own me. I can go where I please." I said as Katt looked at Dai and rolled her eyes. Dai didn't even notice because she was too busy looking at me.

"So, did you move in with him?" Dai asked me.

"He wants me to. But I'm still debating on it. But he did propose to me." I said smiling.

"Oh my god, congrats best friend, when did this happen?" Katt asked me.

"Thank you, and the day I fought Jasmine, well the night." I said smiling.

"So, you're just going to forgive him like that?" Dai asked with an attitude.

"Well yes, Dai you know Giovanni is the love of my life. I can't just let him go like that." I said.

"Whatever, it's always going to be the same thing with y'all. That nigga will never stop cheating and you're always going to end up hurt." She said as she got up and walked towards the door. "Don't forget to lock up." She said as she walked out the door slamming it behind her.

"What's wrong with her?" I asked Katt.

"Girl, I couldn't tell you. But I really am happy for y'all." Katt said.

"Thanks Katt."

"Nanny, where is uncle Gee?" Lil Chris asked me.

"He said he was going to meet up with your father." I said as I sat down on the sofa next to Katt.

"Knowing them two they're probably doing something they don't have no business doing." Katt said as we both laughed.

"Girl you know they are." I said.

"Leese, you look so sick, you're all pale and you're getting fatter." She said looking at me.

"I know, Giovanni told me the same thing this morning before I left. I think I might have a virus or something." I said.

"A virus?" She asked me.

"Yeah, I've been sick since we came back from Michigan Adventures in April." I said.

"Well, you should go to the doctor, it might be something serious." Katt said.

"I am, but I've been busy." I said.

"Busy with what?" Katt asked me.

"Giovanni wants to move, and I've been on the phone with realtors from Cali, Vegas, and ATL." I said sighing.

"Chris asked me did I want to move, but I haven't given an answer yet." Katt said.

"I didn't give Giovanni's ass an answer either. But he said I didn't have a choice." I said laughing.

"That sound like something Gee would say." Katt said as she laughed along with me.

After Katt and I got some clothes we locked the apartment up and then we headed to PF Changs. After we ate, we headed back to our homes. She went to the home she shared with Chris and Lil Chris, and I headed to the home I shared with Giovanni who was sitting on the sofa watching TV when I walked in.

"Where have you been?" He asked me.

"You know I went to the apartment to get some clothes. Then Katt, Lil Chris and I went to PF. And can you get the clothes out the car for me?" I asked him.

"Yeah, I'll get them. And did you tell Katt about the engagement." He asked me.

"I told her and Dai about it." I said as I sat down next to him.

"What did they say?"

"Katt said she was happy for us. But Dai didn't seem like she was happy. She said that it was always going to be the same old thing with us. You weren't going to stop cheating on me and I was always going to end up hurt." I said as I laid my head on his shoulder.

"Baby, I'm not cheating on you anymore. I promise you." He said as he kissed the top off my head. I didn't know if I wanted to trust him or not, but I knew this would be a pointless relationship if I didn't trust him.

Katherine

I was sitting in the living room of the house I now share with Chris and our son wondering what the hell was wrong with Daivon. As of lately, she'd been acting funny around me and Je'leese. I don't think Je'leese had noticed it though. When Je'leese told us about the engagement Daivon looked as if she wanted to cry. I wonder what that was about. "Maybe she's in love with Je'leese." I said aloud to myself. But I was snapped out of my thoughts when my cell phone rang. It was Chris.

"Hello?" I answered.

"What are you up too?" He asked.

"Nothing just put Lil Chris down for his nap about to clean up his room and start dinner." I said.

"I'm glad you decided to move in with me baby." He said.

"I am too. There's no place I'd rather be. Even though I didn't want to leave my girls." I said.

"Baby, Leese and Dai are two grown women. Besides you know Gee is not going to allow Leese to live anywhere besides with him, especially now, since they're engaged. But have you given any more thought to us moving out of state. There's nothing out here for me." He said.

“Moving where?” I asked him.

“Me and Gee have talked about Vegas, Cali, or ATL. You know you and Leese will still be close. And I think Lil Chris would love any of those places.” He said.

“Lil Chris or you?” I asked him.

“What do you mean by that?”

“Nothing Christopher. But what about Dai? I know Leese isn’t going to up and leave her.” I said.

“Baby, Dai is free to do what she wants to do. See that’s you and Leese’s problem now. Y’all are always thinking about Daivon when she’s not thinking about y’all asses. If she had a nigga like me or Gee I’m pretty sure she would have left y’all in that apartment the first chance she got.” He said.

“Baby, I think she’s in love with Leese or something, earlier me and Leese was at the apartment and Leese told us about Gee proposing to her and Dai got mad, like she was really mad. She even walked out the apartment.” I said.

“Baby, something is really wrong with that girl. But I don’t think she likes Leese.” He said.

“When are you coming home?” I asked him changing the subject. I didn’t want to talk about another female that wasn’t doing anything for me or my child.

"I got some business that needs to be handled, but I'll be home with you and my son soon." He said.

"Okay, call me when you're done with your business." I said.

"Okay, I love you baby."

"I love you too Christopher." I said hanging up the phone. After I put my iPhone on the charger I got up and started to clean up. There wasn't really anything that needed to be done besides the laundry and the kitchen because I cooked breakfast this morning. I went in Lil Chris' room so I could wash his clothes first. Then I did me and Christopher's clothes; while I was doing that, I started the dishes and dinner.

Jasmine

I was sitting in Gee's driveway deciding if I wanted to go knock on the door. I knew his girl was in there because her car was parked right next to his. So I knew getting some money and dick was out of the question. My eye was back to normal, but my damn nose was still hurting me every day. I didn't want to knock on the door just in case she answered the door and punched my ass again. I turned my car off, but left my keys in the ignition then I walked up to Gee's door. I knocked twice before his girl opened the door.

"What the hell do you want?" She asked. I wanted to run the hell away from the door right then and there.

"Um, is Giovanni here?" I asked her with a huge lump in my throat.

"His is namc is Gee to you. And what do you want with him?" She asked just as Gee walked up behind her.

"What the fuck are you doing here?" He asked me.

"I came here to warn you." I said.

"Warn him about what?" Je'leese asked me.

"Dora is planning on trapping you." I said ignoring the bitch.

"What the hell you mean? And who is Dora?" Je'leese asked looking from me to Gee.

"Leesy, go back in the house. I'll explain it to you later." Gee said looking at her.

"Giovanni, I'm not going anywhere. Who the hell is Dora, and what does this hoe mean she's trying to trap you?" She asked.

"Dora is a hoe that I use to fuck with. She came after you and Jasmine fought and said that she was pregnant by me. But I knew the hoe was lying, because every hoe I hit I wore a condom. Ask Jasmine." Gee said. Je'leese ignored him and turned her attention to me.

"Look hoe, what do you know?" She asked me.

"Look girl, I didn't come over here to start anything with you. But if you keep calling me out my name…" I started but she interrupted me.

"What the fuck are you gone do bitch? Didn't I beat yo ass already? Now, I suggest you either tell me what the fuck you know or get the fuck on." She said.

Shit, I turned my ass around and walked towards my car. I couldn't fight; all my ass could do was talk shit. As soon as I got in my car I turned the keys in the ignition and pulled out the driveway.

I drove around the city of Detroit with no destination. Then I decided to go check up on my cousin in Southwest. It was a long drive so I stopped at the next gas station I saw to fill my tank up and grab me something to snack on. Then I was on my way.

When I got to Southwest everybody and their mama was sitting outside. It was the summer and the sun was shining bright. My windows were rolled down, and I smiled. Every nigga that was outside was looking into my car. But I didn't give them eye contact. I drove down Bassett and pulled into my cousin's baby's daddy's parent's driveway.

"Well, look what the wind blew in." She said from the porch.

"How have you been Brandy?" I asked her getting out my car.

"Girl, you know I've been straight. Just trying to live," Brandy said.

"How is Brandon?" I asked her.

"He's fine. Running around here being bad with his brothers." She said.

"You and James aren't back together?" I asked her.

"Girl, no. This nigga done got another hoe pregnant." She said.

"How many is it now?" I asked.

"He's got four now, and three on the way." Brandy said.

"Damn, does this nigga even believe in condoms?" I asked her shaking my head.

"I don't think so." She said as she grabbed a blunt from the astray that was sitting at her feet.

"So, when are we going out again?" I asked.

"Whenever." She said as she lit the blunt.

"Um, you know Summer Jams and River Days are at the end of this month right?" I asked her.

"Oh yeah, I haven't been to either of those in some years." She said.

"Girl my ass go every year. Especially Summer Jams. Last year they had Young Jeezy, this year they gone have MMG, Avant and some more people." I said as she passed me the blunt.

"How much are the tickets?" She asked me.

"Don't worry about it. I'll buy yours. And pay for you to get into River Days." I said.

“Aw, you’re the best cousin in the world.” She said as her baby’s daddy’s sister Candice walked on the porch.

“Wassup Jass?” She said to me.

“Hey Candice, what’s up with you?” I asked her.

“Nothing girl, I’m just getting off work. How you been?” She asked me.

“Girl, I’ve been good. You still working at McDonalds?” I asked her.

“Yes and they’re working me like a damn slave.” She said.

“We should all go out this weekend. They’re having an after party for Yo Gotti and J. Cole.” Brandy said to both Candice and me.

“That sounds like a plan. But I need to see what this weak ass baby daddy of mine gone do about his son.” She said as she walked into the house.

“Girl, don’t James’ parents get tired of y’all?” I asked her shaking my head. Brandy, Candice, and Candice’s three older sisters Courtney, Cherri, and Bianca all lived with their parents, along with their kids.

“I don’t know. They never tell me anything.” She said as my phone beeped. It was a text message from this dude name Mike that I use to mess with.

"Aye, I'm on my way to yo crib. I need to lay low." He said.

"Girl, I need to go. Comcast is coming over to fix my cable." I lied as I looked up from my phone.

"Alright, girl, call me later." She said as I got up and walked off the porch and towards my car.

"Okay." I said as I got in my car and started it up.

Chris

It was going on six o'clock and I was pulling into the parking lot behind the building that Ashley lives in. I had to come see this hoe before she sent Katt some more pictures of me and my daughter Christina. I didn't know how this hoe got Katt's number. I got out the car and walked towards the front of the building Ashley was sitting outside with her cousin Dora.

"Well, well, well." Ashley said as I walked straight past them and into the house. My daughter was sitting in the middle of the floor playing with her baby doll and watching TV.

"Daddy!" Christina screamed as she dropped the doll she was playing with and ran to me.

"Hey baby girl, how are you?" I asked her.

"I'm fine daddy. I just miss you a lot. I wanna go home with you." Christina said.

"I miss you too baby. Don't you like being over here with your mommy?" I asked her.

"No daddy, she yells at me all the time. I want to live with you." She said and I instantly got mad. I didn't want anyone yelling at my kids. Katt doesn't even yell at Lil Chris when he does something wrong. And I doubted Christina had done anything wrong. So I'd be damned if Ashley yelled at my only daughter.

"Go in your room baby girl, I'll be in there in a minute." I said.

"Okay." She said as I put her down. She grabbed her doll then walked into her room.

"Ashley!" I called out as I sat down on the sofa. "Ashley!" I said again just as she walked into the apartment.

"What the hell are you yelling for?" She asked.

"Why my daughter don't like being around yo ass? And why the fuck are you yelling at her? I'm pretty sure she don't be doing shit to yo ass." I said.

"My daughter loves being around me. Her ass just need to start listening and maybe I won't yell at her." She said.

"My fucking daughter don't like being around you. She just told me she don't want to live here and she wants to live with me." I said.

"But is she going to live with you? Hell no! So what the fuck are you telling me this for?" She asked. But before I could answer she continued. "You're keeping my fucking daughter in the dark because you cheated and don't want to lose your girl, but you haven't thought about how it affects Christina. She's with me every damn day and all she can talk about is seeing her daddy, and her daddy this or her daddy that. Do you think she ever thinks about her mommy?" She asked.

"Well, if you weren't too busy being a fucking whore and going to the fucking club every damn day then maybe she would think about yo simple minded ass." I said as I got up off the sofa and walked into my daughter's room. When I got in there it was a damn mess. There was clothes, and toys everywhere. That just made me even madder, I wanted to go out there and choke Ashley's ass.

"Am I going with you daddy?" She asked me as I grabbed her princess bag off the door and started packing her some clothes that was in the dresser.

"Yes baby. Put your shoes on and grab your doll." I said as I zipped up the bag. She smiled. When we walked out the room Ashley was standing where I left her.

"Where the hell are you taking my daughter?" She asked me as she stood in front of the door.

"Watch your mouth in front of my daughter, and get out my way." I said grabbing Christina's hand.

"Chris, where are you taking my daughter?" She asked again placing her hands on her hips.

"She's going with her daddy. Where, is none of your business. Now get out of my way." I said. She moved out my way and we walked out the door and to my car. I made sure Christina had her seat belt on before I got in the driver's seat. I sat there for a minute thinking about what I was going to do now that I had Christina with me.

Daivon

I can't believe this nigga Gee asked Je'leese to marry him. I was already pissed off that the nigga took my brand new iPhone 5 and did lord knows what with it; so finding that out made me madder. But the day after he took it I went to Sprint and got me that new Galaxy. Now I was just sitting on the sofa wondering when he proposed to Je'leese, as I sat there thinking he must have done it before he came to see me. So that was the reason he got to my room quick as hell, he was already at the hotel. I grabbed my phone and scrolled down until I found Gee's number. He wasn't about to marry that bitch if I had anything to do with it.

"Gee, we need to talk." I texted him. After I sent that text I put my phone on the sofa then walked into the kitchen. After I grabbed me something to drink I walked back into the living room grabbed my phone then walked into my room. When I got in there I had a message.

Gee texted back, ***"Bitch, do you not speak English or some shit? Didn't I tell yo ass don't fucking call or text me anymore? What the fuck is wrong with you?"***

"Yo ass is what's wrong with me. But it's cool. You either tell Je'leese about us or I will." I texted back.

"Bitch I ain't telling her shit, and neither are you." He texted back.

"Yeah okay! We're going to see." I texted back, but as soon as I put the phone down on the bed his ass was calling.

"Hello?" I answered smiling.

"Bitch, what type of games are you trying to play?" He asked me.

"Nigga, you heard what I said. It's either you tell her or I'll tell her. It's up to you. I'll give you until the day after Summer Jams to figure out what you want to do." I said hanging up the phone. And I was serious; he had a few weeks to decide what the fuck he wanted to do. But either way Je'leese was going to find out about us, and Katherine was going to find out about me fucking Chris, and none of them would be getting married. I sat on my bed thinking about the night I had a threesome with Gee and Chris. They both were drunk and I was sober. I spiked their drink one night after a party and texted Gee pretending to be Katt telling him that I needed him and Chris to meet me at the Marriot downtown. They both came. When they saw me on the bed naked as the day I came into the world they couldn't resist me. They both were horny and their dicks were standing at full attention. I got off the bed and pulled both of them further into the room. While I was fucking Gee I had Chris take pictures of us, and while I was fucking Chris I had Gee take pictures of us. Gee got in one of the double beds that was in the room, and Chris got in the other one. Once

Gee was sleep I climbed in the bed with him, I guess he thought I was Je'leese because he pulled me closer to him. But when he woke up the next morning I thought he was going to kill me. I told them what happened, but I didn't tell them about me drugging them. I just told them I texted them and told them to meet me at the hotel and they came. Once they got in the room they weren't trying to leave. I had a smile on my face just thinking about how Chris and Gee blew my back out.

Giovanni

Je'leese still had an attitude with me since Jasmine came over here telling me about Dora's crazy ass. She was upstairs in our room lying down, and I was sitting downstairs thinking of ways I could keep Daivon's crazy ass from telling Je'leese what happened between us. She was texting my phone talking some crazy shit earlier. I cursed myself for having such good dick that kept these hoes hooked. I got up from the sofa and was walking towards the stairs when my mans Chris called me. I turned back around and headed towards the kitchen.

"Hello?" I said.

"Man, where you at?" He asked me.

"The crib with Leese. Why, what's up?" I asked him.

"Man, that dirty bitch Ashley sent Katt some pictures the night Leese fucked Jasmine up." He said.

"Damn, how thc hell did she get Katt number? But that exact same day that bitch Dora came over here talking about she pregnant." I said.

"I couldn't even tell you how that bitch got her number. But you know Katt work at Greenfield Plaza, so it ain't that hard. And that bitch Dora is at Ashley's house right now. I had to go over there to see my daughter, but I ended up taking her with me. She didn't want to be with her mama." He said.

"Damn bro, what the hell are you going to do?" I asked him.

"I don't even know. Katt and Lil Chris are at my house. I don't want to lie to her, but I don't want to tell her the truth. Well at least not right now." He said.

"You know we don't lie to them, that's rule number one. Never lie to the main, they don't deserve that. If you're going to lie to anybody let it be them hoes. Either tell her the truth or take Christina to your parent's house." I told him.

"You right bro. What's going on with you and that Daivon situation?" He asked me.

"That bitch texted me talking about I got until the day after Summer Jams to tell Leese or she gone tell her." I said shaking my head.

"Man, these hoes really losing their minds." He said.

"Tell me about it. But look let me hit you back later. I need to handle some things with Leese." I said.

"Ight, but can you do me a favor?" He asked me.

"What's up?" I asked him.

"Do you want to Christen Stina?" He asked me.

“I’d be honored too bro.” I said.

“Fasho bro, and congratulations on the engagement.” He said.

“Good looking fool.” I said hanging up the phone. When I got in the room Je’leese was in the bathroom that was connected to the room, she was once again on the floor with her face in the toilet.

“Leesy, if you’re sick why not go to the doctor?” I asked her.

“I’m fine.” She snapped as she got up to brush her teeth and wash her face.

“Why are you so mad? I told you I’m not messing with them hoes anymore.” I said as she walked out the bathroom, I followed her.

“Can you please stop talking to me?” She asked.

“No, I’m not gone stop talking to you. What is your problem?” I asked her.

“There is no problem Giovanni, I just have a headache.” She said as she got back in the bed. I took my shirt off and climbed into the bed next to her.

“I’m sorry, I just thought you were mad at me.” I said as I pulled her body closer to mine.

"I'm not mad Giovanni. I don't have the strength to be mad at you right now." She said.

"Leesy, I know I put you through a lot of shit, but baby girl you gotta know I'm sorry." I said.

"I know Giovanni." She said as she looked me in my eyes. "What are we going to do for our anniversary?" She asked me.

"We've been together, what eight years?" I asked.

"Yes, it doesn't feel like it though." She said.

"I know, but I'm glad you put up with me for so long. Are you going to set a date?" I asked her.

"Set a date for what?" She asked me.

"Je'leese, didn't I just give you a ring? I didn't give it to you just for show. I gave it to you for a reason." I said looking into her eyes.

"I know baby, I just didn't think you'd want to get married so soon." She said.

"Baby girl, we can get married tomorrow. You know I'm ready." I said.

"I want a small ceremony. You know I don't have any family besides Katt and Daivon." She said. I rolled my eyes.

"Well, whatever you want you know you got it." I said as I kissed the top of her head.

"I know you do. And you know I got your back." She said.

"Oh really? You gone ride or die?" I asked already knowing the answer.

"Haven't I proven that several times?" She asked as she pulled away from me and looked at my face.

"Yes baby, you have proven that several times." I said smiling.

"Well, at least you know no matter what I'm gone ride. But you also should know if I find out you still cheating I'm gone shoot the bitch you cheating with, and I just might kill yo ass." She said with a smile, but I knew she was serious.

"Don't worry about it baby. I'm giving up that life. You're the only woman I want to be with in every way." I said as she climbed on top of my body.

"That's good to know." She said as she started to kiss me.

Katherine

I was sitting on the sofa waiting on Christopher to come home; it was now past the time he told me he'd be home. So now I was mad. I turned off the TV just as my phone rang. It was Je'leese.

"Hello." I said.

"Wassup Bestie?" She asked.

"Nothing, waiting on Christopher's ass. What are you up too?"

"What are y'all about to do? And nothing, just laying here with Giovanni." She said as we both laughed.

"Nothing at all. That nigga is in the dog house, I cooked for me, him and Lil Chris and he didn't make it home. But did Gee mention something else about moving?" I asked her.

"Girl yes, he was talking that bullshit the other night. Why? Did Chris say something else about it?" She asked.

"Yes, he said that he and Gee was looking into moving too Cali, ATL, or Vegas. But he don't want Daivon to come." I said.

"Gee said the same thing, I wonder what's up with that."

"I do too, but something is wrong with her. She's been acting a little funny lately." I replied.

"She's just sad because we both have men in our lives and she doesn't have anyone." Leese said.

"Leese, that's her own fault. We've had Gee and Chris in our lives for eight years now. I think it's time for her to either find a man of her own or get over being mad, jealous, or whatever it is."

"I know what you saying. Maybe we should talk to her about it." She said.

"Yeah, just let me know when you're ready." I said.

"Okay, but Giovanni wants me to get off this phone. I'll call you in the morning."

"Okay girl, tell Gee I said hey."

"I will, and tell Lil Chris and big Chris I said hey." She said.

"Okay." I said hanging up the phone. I turned the TV off, went into the kitchen, and put the food in the fridge. After that I walked up the stairs to check on my son. Then I went to the room I shared with Christopher. I dialed his number and it went straight to voicemail. I threw my phone on the bed, grabbed my iPod off the nightstand, and put the headphones in. The first song that came on was Meek Mill "Dreams & Nightmares". I loved all his songs, but right now this was by far my favorite.

I fell asleep listening to music, but when I opened my eyes Christopher was walking into the room.

"Sorry I'm late. I stopped by my parents crib." He said as he walked into the closet.

"Yeah whatever." I said.

"What you mad for?" He asked me as he turned around to face me.

"Because, we were supposed to have family dinner, but you were so busy doing other things that you didn't make it." I said as I paused my music.

"It's not like that Katt." He said.

"Then what's it like Christopher?" I asked him.

"You know I'm doing what I do for you and my son." He said.

"No, you're doing what you do for your damn self. Me and Lil Chris have nothing to do with it." I said.

"Come on Katherine, can we talk about this another time? I'm tired." He said.

"We don't have to talk about it anymore. I'm going to sleep in one of the guest rooms." I said as I grabbed my iPod and iPhone and walked out the room.

Daivon

For the next few days I did nothing but lay in my bed and shop. I was mad as hell because Katt and Leese kept their doors locked. I wanted to do a little snooping. I was walking around the house when my cell phone rang. It was my sperm donor David.

"Hello." I answered with an attitude.

"Hey baby girl. How is everything going with you?" He asked me.

"Why? Don't act like you give a fuck what's going on me with me." I replied

"Daivon, watch your mouth when you're talking to me. No matter how much you hate me I'm still your father." He snapped.

"If you're such a damn father, then you wouldn't have left my mother for a white bitch. You're nothing but a sperm donor to me. Now what do you want?" I asked him.

"I was just calling to tell you Janice and I will be in town for River Days at the end of this month and your little sister Danielle will also be there." David said.

"Okay, and your point of telling me this was? I don't want to see you, your wife, nor y'all child. I don't have any siblings." I said hanging up the phone. When I got back in my room I sat on my bed and my phone started ringing again. It was David again.

"What do you want?" I answer irritated.

"Daivon, I'm sorry for how things transpired, but I think we really should talk." David said.

"There's nothing to talk about David. We could have talked before you cheated on mama for a white woman. But you didn't want to talk, did you? You didn't even come see me when you moved out. All you cared about was your wife and your precious Danielle." I said as tears rolled down my face.

"Dai, that's not true, I just had to be there for Danny. She was sick and needed me." David said.

"No, I needed you but you didn't care, did you? Just stop calling my phone. I don't want anything to do with you." I said hanging up the phone. This time I cut it off. I looked at my night stand at the last photo me and my mother took together. It was at my thirteenth birthday party. She was smiling, but she had stress written all over her face. Who would have known that she would kill herself just ten minutes after that picture was taken? I picked the picture up and held it in my hands.

"Mommy, I miss you so much. I need you here with me!" I said as the tears continued to roll down my face. The only time I cry is when I'm thinking about my mother. I really did need her here with me. I wouldn't have to worry about black-mailing Gee. I wouldn't have to worry about Je'leese or Katherine. Of course, I was mad at my mother for leaving like she did. But I understood her pain. I wanted both Chris and Gee. Since I knew I couldn't have either of them, no one could. It was so much easier getting what I wanted from Gee because he would do anything to keep Je'leese with him; he cared about her feelings and didn't like to hurt them. Chris on the other hand, I think he's with Katt because of their son Lil Chris. I don't know why that bitch didn't understand that. But both Chris and Gee hated my guts. But soon Je'leese and Katt were going to hate their guts.

Jasmine

I haven't seen nor spoken to Gee since the day I went to his house. And I was really having withdrawals from his dick. Maybe it was just dick period. I thought I was going to get some from Mike's ass but his ass went straight to sleep as soon as he sat down on the sofa. When he woke up I'd asked him why was he so sleepy, he said he'd been trapping all night and when he got home his baby mama was tripping and he didn't want to hear that shit. Dora had been blowing up my phone. But I was sending the bitch straight to voicemail. We didn't have shit to talk about. I was walking out my door headed to the Sprint store so I could buy me a new phone and change my number when I saw Dora and Ashley walking up. Shit. I said in my head.

"What's up?" I asked them, well I asked Dora.

"Why haven't you been answering your phone? I've been trying to get in touch with you." Dora said.

"I dropped my phone in some water, I was just on my way to Sprint so I can get a new one." I said.

"I wanted you to call Gee and ask him had he talked to me." Dora said. This bitch must really be stupid.

"Dora, didn't I just say I dropped my phone in some water?" I asked her with a bit of attitude in my voice.

"Dora, I don't even know why you fuck with this bitch." Ashley said.

"Ash chill out, Jas will you do it once you get another phone?" She asked me.

"Yeah, but I need to get going before Sprint close." I said.

"Okay, call me later." She said as she walked towards her car and I walked towards mine. I was going to call Gee, but it wasn't going to be for that bitch. It was going to be for me. I needed some dick in my life and I didn't want any from Mike, at least not right now.

After I got my new phone and got back in my car I dialed Gee's number. It rang four times before he finally answered it.

"Hello." He said in a groggy voice.

"Were you sleep?" I asked him.

"Nah, who is this?" He asked.

"Jas." I said.

"Look Jas, Je'leese and I are engaged. I'm done fucking around on her. Stop calling and texting my phone." He said.

"I'm pregnant!" I blurted out. It wasn't true. But he wasn't going to drop me like that.

"Jasmine, go play with somebody else. Don't call me anymore." He said.

"Alright, we gone see when this baby get here." I said, but he hung up in my face. I looked at the screen then called back five times. But he didn't answer none of the calls, so I texted him.

"How will your fiancée feel when she finds out that you have a baby on the way?" I texted. Not even two minutes later he called.

"Hello." I said smiling.

"Jasmine? I know Giovanni just asked you not to call or text him anymore. And this is the only warning I will be giving out. If you ever call or text him again, I promise you, I will find you and put my foot in your ass." Je'leese said. That shit sent chills down my spine. I didn't say anything. "I know yo ass hear me. Just don't call Giovanni anymore." She said hanging up the phone. I sat there for like ten minutes with the phone stuck to my ear.

Je'leese

I don't know what Giovanni has been doing to these little females because they are really losing their minds. I was really trying to figure out what the hell was going on. There were two different bitches calling and texting his phone claiming that they were pregnant and he was the daddy. He said that he never ran up in them raw, but I had my doubts. I never let him know that though. But my ass has been sick for like three months now. I think I got some sort of stomach virus. I think I really got it when Giovanni and I went to Michigan Adventures. For a few weeks, all I was able to eat was saltine crackers, and drink orange juice. I was happy that I was able to eat real food now.

"Baby, I think you should really go see the doctor." Giovanni said as I walked into the kitchen where he was cooking breakfast.

"I'm fine Giovanni. I don't need to see a doctor." I said as I sat down on the table.

"Really Je'leese? You throw up every damn day. You can't even keep food down, and you don't need to see a doctor? Who do you think you're lying to?" He asked.

"Just let it go. I'm fine." I said as he brought the plate over and sat it in front of me. The eggs, grits, sausages, and biscuits looked so good, but when I inhaled it I had to throw up. I got up from the table and ran into the bathroom.

"See what I'm saying?" Giovanni said to me as he ran behind me. I didn't even make it to the bathroom this time; I threw up in the hallway. Giovanni just looked away.

"I'll clean it up." I said as I stepped over it and walked towards the cleaning closet that was in the kitchen.

"Nah, I got it. Go clean yourself up. I'll bring you some soup up." He said.

"Are you sure?" I asked him.

"Yes I'm sure Je'leese." He said giving me an impatient look. I wanted to kiss him, but I didn't. I just walked past him and walked up the stairs. When I got in the room I walked into the bathroom, turned on the shower and stripped out of my clothes. I brushed my teeth as I waited for the water to warm up.

"Something's gotta give with this sickness." I said aloud to myself.

After my shower I was laying in the bed watching BET when my cell phone rang. It was Dai.

"Hello." I said.

"Hey girl, you must have forgotten about me." She said.

"You know I can never forget about you. What have you been doing?" I asked her.

"Nothing, sitting in this boring house by myself." She said.

"Aw, I'm sorry for leaving you there by yourself. I'm going to see if Giovanni will let you come spend some time over here." I said as Giovanni walked into the room.

"Girl, you sound like a little kid." Dai said laughing.

"Who is that?" He asked me.

"Dai." I said.

"Hell no, she can't come over here." He said, I tried to cover up the mouth piece but she still heard what he said.

"That's okay. How about me, you, and Katt meet up for dinner or something?" She said.

"That's fine, just call me later and tell me where to meet you." I said.

"Okay, call Katt and see if she's free." She said.

"Okay." I said hanging up the phone.

"Here," he said as he handed me a tray with soup, crackers, and a bottle of orange juice.

"What is wrong with you?" I asked him.

"What are you talking about?" He asked as he got in the bed.

"Dai is over there lonely, I don't like her being alone." I said.

"Well tell her lonely ass to get a damn man, or even better a damn puppy. Her ass ain't coming to my house." He said laughing.

"So, your lil hoes can come to the house but she can't?" I asked him.

"This don't have shit to do with those hoes. She can't come to my house, and that's final." He said.

"Why?" I asked him, but he didn't answer me. He just picked up the remote and turned the TV up. I wanted to smack that damn remote out his hand, and smack his ass while I was at it. Instead, I sat the tray on my nightstand and got off the bed. I walked into the walk-in closet and got me a Nike outfit from the top shelf and put it on.

"Where are you going?" He asked as I walked out the closet. I didn't answer him. I grabbed some socks from the dresser and picked up my Nike gym shoes and put them on. After I had on my shoes I grabbed my phone and walked out the room. Once I got downstairs I sat down in the living room and dialed Katt's number.

Katherine

I was just getting out the shower when I heard my phone ringing; I picked it up off the bed and looked at it. It was Je'leese.

"Hello." I said.

"What are you doing?" She asked me.

"I'm just getting out the shower. What's wrong?" I asked her, I knew something was wrong with her just by the tone in her voice.

"Giovanni just pissed me off. Can you please come get me?" She asked me.

"Yeah, let me put on my clothes then I'll be on my way."

"Okay, thank you."

"Your welcome." I said as I hung up the phone. Once I had my clothes on I called Chris who had taken Lil Chris to see his grandparents.

"Hello." He answered.

"Where are you at?" I asked him.

"The Mile, what up?" I asked him.

“What the hell you doing on the Mile? I know damn well your parents don’t live on Seven Mile.” I said.

“Baby calm down. I had to check on the shops, but what’s up you need something?” He asked me.

“Nope, but I’m going to pick up Leese, her and Gee got into it again.” I said.

“Okay, do you need me to holla at my boy?” He asked me.

“No, I doubt it was that serious, when she called me she sounded like they were just arguing.” I said.

“Alright, well call me later.”

“Mhm, and you better hurry up and get off the Mile, I know you got some hoes that stay over there.” I said as I grabbed my keys and umbrella for the rain; then I walked out the door.

“Come on Katt, I’m not over here for no hoes.” He said.

“Whatever, but I’ll call you later.” I said.

“Aight, I love you.” He said.

“I love you too Christopher.” I said as I got in my car.

When I got to Gee’s house, I got out the car and walked to the door. I heard Gee and Leese arguing.

"I don't even care anymore Giovanni. Just stop talking to me right now." Je'leese said.

"Leesy, you getting mad over something so damn petty. I'm pretty sure Chris don't want Daivon's ass in his house neither." I heard Gee said. I knocked on the door before they could go any further.

"Come in." Je'leese said. I opened the door and walked in. Je'leese and Gee were standing toe to toe. Even though Gee was at least three feet taller than her, she was still holding her own.

"Is everything okay?" I asked.

"Yeah, everything straight." Gee said as he walked away.

"Can we go?" Je'leese asked me.

"Yeah, come on." I said.

"Bye Leese." Gee said, Je'leese ignored him. When we got in the car Je'leese looked as if she was going to cry.

"Are you okay?" I asked her.

"Yeah, I'm fine." She said. I heard the sadness all in her voice. I wanted to say something that would make her feel better, but I didn't know what to say.

Jasmine

After Gee's bitch answered the phone I didn't even want to call or text him anymore. Dora called me later that night on my house phone and asked me did I get in touch with him, and I told her ass no. She said he hadn't been answering her phone calls either. I was happy about that. But I wasn't happy about him marrying that bitch. I was sitting on my patio smoking on some loud when my phone rang. I was happy when I saw it was Gee.

"Hello." I said as I put the blunt down.

"What you doing?" He asked me.

"Nothing, didn't you say you was done with me?" I asked him.

"Look, don't question me. But are you trying to meet me?" He asked.

"Where? Can't I just come to your house?" I asked him.

"My girl lives with me now, you know that. We can meet somewhere down town and get a room at Greektown." He said.

"Gee, do you know how much those rooms cost?" I asked him.

“Did I ask you anything about how much they cost? Look if you not down to meet me just say that instead of wasting my time.” He said.

“I’ll meet you!” I yelled out quickly.

“Good, give me about an hour then meet me at Hart Plaza.” He said hanging up the phone. I was so geeked that he wanted to see me that I finished off the blunt then got in the shower.

I took more than an hour in the shower, so I had to rush to fix my hair and do my makeup. I only had ten minutes to get downtown. When I was finally done with my hair and makeup, I ran out the door and to my car. Once I was in my car I turned the radio on and they were playing Rocko ‘U.O.E.N.O.’

“Jasmine still fucking Gee and Je’leese ont even know.” I said aloud as I laughed. In my mind I was scared; I thought this could be a set up. But I dismissed the thought just as quickly as it came to my mind.

Even though it was raining, Hart Plaza and the River Walk were still full of people. I was standing in the middle of Hart Plaza looking for Gee when my phone rang.

“Hello.” I answered.

“Yo, where you at?”

“Hart Plaza, where are you?” I asked him.

“Where you parked yo car at?” He asked me.

“In the Marriott parking lot.” I said.

“Alright, meet me there.” He said hanging up the phone. I turned around and walked towards the Marriott.

“Jasmine.” I heard somebody say. I turned around and Dora was standing there with Ashley and Ashley’s sister Asia.

“Oh, hey Dora.” I said in a dry tone.

“Where are you going?” She asked.

“Oh, I was supposed to meet up with my cousin Brandy and her sister-in-law Candice. But they couldn’t make it.” I lied.

“Well why don’t you just hang out with us?” Dora asked. Ashley looked as if she wanted to say something, but she didn’t.

“No thanks, maybe another time. I’m tired.” I said.

“Are you sure?” Dora asked me.

“Yeah, but call me later. Maybe we can go out later or something.” I said.

“Okay.” She said. Ashley and Asia rolled their eyes at me, as I walked away, well more like ran.

"What took you so long?" Gee asked leaning against my car.

"I ran into your little girlfriend." I said.

"Je'leese?" He asked standing up straight and looking around.

"No, Dora." I said smiling.

"That's not my fucking girlfriend, na open the door." He snapped. I did as he said and we both got into the car.

Daivon

I was walking around Northland Mall when I heard somebody call my name. I turned around to see who it was, and it was this nigga Tim I use to date.

"What's up?" I asked him when he got closer to me.

"Shit, I'm trying to see what's up with yo fine ass." Tim said as he pulled me into a hug. I couldn't lie, he smelled so good and it turned me on.

"Ain't nothing. But I miss you." I said.

"I miss you more girl, you know I was in love with yo ass until you broke my heart." He said smiling, but I knew he was serious.

"I did not break yo heart." I said laughing.

"Yes you did ma. I was gone ask you to marry me until you just upped and said you wasn't happy." He said, and that was true, I wasn't happy. I broke things off with him two weeks after I fucked Gee and Chris. I wanted to be happy with one of them.

"You know I'm sorry about that, but I wasn't happy. You were always too busy with the game and didn't realize I was at home waiting on you." I said.

"I'm sorry about that ma, but look. I gotta get my mama this dress before she miss Bingo, I gotta tell her I ran into you. But do you want to do dinner or something tonight?" He asked me.

"I would, but I'm doing dinner with Katt and Leese, we can do a night cap though." I said smiling.

"Okay, we can do that. Put your number in my phone." He said. We both pulled our phones out. I dialed my number from his phone so I could have his number too. I then walked through the mall so I could shop. I was in Victoria's Secret when my phone rang. It was Je'leese.

"Wassup?" I asked her.

"Hey Dai, where are you?" She asked, and it sounded like she had been crying.

"I'm at the mall. Why, what's up?" I asked.

"I was just asking so are we still on for tonight?"

"Yeah, I got a taste for some Sweetwater, so y'all down?" I asked her.

"Yeah, what time?"

"Um, say around seven. I got a date with Tim around nine." I told her.

"Aw snap, y'all back talking?" She asked.

"I just ran into him at the mall and he asked me did I want to do something later tonight." I said.

"Well, let me get off this phone and get ready. I'll see you in a few." She said.

"Okay." I said hanging up the phone. I looked at the time and realized it was already five thirty. After I got what I wanted from the mall, I left and headed back to the apartment so I could get dressed. Once I was dressed, I packed an overnight bag because I was more than likely going to spend the night out with Tim.

Chris

I was riding around Detroit thinking of a way to tell Katt about Christina without her wanting to leave me or take Lil Chris from me. I didn't want to lie to her. But I didn't know how to tell her the truth either. Lil Chris met Christina when I dropped him off over my parent's house. I told them that they were brother and sister. I also told Lil Chris he couldn't tell his mama because it was a surprise. Lil Chris and Christina played so well together whenever Lil Chris was over my parent's crib where Christina was staying. She was shy around him for a few minutes until I told her that Lil Chris was her big brother and he was going to protect her like I'll protect her. Christina is a shy child, and don't like meeting new people. It took her days to warm up to my mama and daddy. But they won her over in the end. I was so caught up in my thoughts that I almost didn't hear my phone ringing. I looked at the screen and saw it was my nigga Gee.

"What's popping my nigga?" I asked him.

"Come scoop me."

"Where you at nigga?"

"Greektown." He said.

"With who?"

"That hoe Jasmine, my car is in front of the Coney around the corner from Sweetwater." He replied.

"Aight, I'm on my way now." I said.

"Fasho my nigga." He said as we both hung up the phone. Good thing I was already heading his way. It was going to take me less than fifteen minutes to get to where he was. While riding I was listening to the radio and they said something about Summer Jams and River Days. Both Lil Chris and Christina talked about going. I didn't know if I was going to take them though or if I even wanted them to go.

When I got to Greektown, Gee was standing outside waiting on me.

"Man that hoe play too fucking much." He said looking down at his phone.

"What she do?" I asked.

"Talking about she really is pregnant. You should have saw the look I gave her. But I hit her off with six hundred and told her if she was really pregnant to get an abortion." He said as I laughed.

"Man, yo ass crazy."

"I'm serious. I don't have time for that baby mama drama. Especially seeing what you go through with Ashley. Plus I still gotta deal with that crazy bitch Daivon." He said.

"So, what's going on with y'all?" I asked him.

"Shit, I haven't fucked her since the night Je'leese fought Jasmine. She's been calling me and shit, but I send the bitch straight to voicemail."

"So, when are you trying to move up outta this state? I'm ready to leave like ASAP." I said.

"You told Katt about Stina?" He asked me.

"Nah man, I don't even know how to tell her some shit like that." He said.

"Man, let's take them to the Coleman A center Thursday and marry them." He said all of a sudden.

"Are you serious?" I asked him.

"Hell yeah, man neither one of them have any family. My parents are dead so let's just invite your folks and they can be our witnesses. Hell we already got the wedding bands." He said.

"Alright man, I like that idea." I said as I turned down Congress.

"Ain't that Katt's car?" He asked me.

"Where?" I asked him.

"Right there in Sweetwater's parking lot." He said.

"Hell yeah!" I said as I pulled into the parking lot and pulled up next to her.

Je'leese

I couldn't even enjoy this time with my best friends because my mind was so cloudy with thoughts about Giovanni and how mad he made me this morning.

"What's up with you Leese?" Dai asked. I didn't want to tell her that she was the reason me and Giovanni got into it this morning.

"Nothing, I just don't feel good." I said, and that was some of the truth.

"Did you go to the doctors?" She asked me.

"No, I don't think it's that serious." I said. Katt looked at me but didn't say anything.

"Are you sure?" Dai asked me.

"Yes." I said.

"So, about this date you have with Tim." Katt said, and I knew she was trying to take the pressure off me.

"He made me feel bad about breaking his heart." Dai said.

"Why did you break his heart again?" I asked her laughing as I took a sip of my water.

“Because he didn’t know how to make me happy. How are you and Gee?” She asked.

“We’re fine.” I said smiling.

“So, y’all are still planning on getting married?” She asked. She was so busy looking at her plate that she didn’t notice the look Katt gave me.

“Yes we are. Why are you asking me all these questions?” I asked her.

“I was just asking. I’m your best friend, I just want to make sure you’re happy.” She said never taking her eyes off her plate.

“Dai, you know I’m happy. And I wouldn’t be happy with anybody else.” I said.

“Well, you being happy is the only thing that matters, right?” She asked.

“Yeah, I guess.” I said.

“Leesy, can we talk?” Giovanni asked from behind me. I turned around to see him and Chris standing there.

“Sure.” I said as I got up and followed him. He walked outside and stood next to Chris’ car.

“How did you know I was here?” Was the first question out of my mouth.

"I was riding pass with Chris and I saw Katt's car." He said.

"How did you know that it was Katt's car and not somebody else car?"

"As many times as I done seen that car. And besides, Chris know his girl car."

"What do you want? And where is your car?" I asked him.

"I'm sorry for earlier, I just don't want Daivon in my house. And it's at the Coney. Me and Chris had to handle some business." He replied.

"She's been there before so why can't she just come over again?" I asked.

"Baby, just listen to me this one time okay? I don't want her in my house. The only female that can come over my house besides you is Katt." He said.

"Giovanni, I don't understand this, but whatever." I said not wanting to argue with him anymore.

"Can you say you forgive me?" He asked.

"I forgive you Giovanni." I said.

"Did you eat anything in there?" He asked me.

“I had a few fries, and a couple bites of chicken.” I said as Dai, Katt, and Chris walked towards us. “What’s up?” I asked them.

“Dai is going to be late for her date, and Chris and I have to pick Lil Chris up from his parent’s house before it gets too late.” Katt said.

“Okay, call me later.” I said to Dai.

“Do you need a ride to your car?” Chris asked Giovanni.

“Naw, me and my baby about to enjoy a walk.” Giovanni said as he grabbed my hand and we started to walk towards Jefferson.

Katherine

I was driving my car to the house while Chris followed behind me so we could drop my car off and I could get in the car with him then go get Lil Chris. When we got to the house, Chris ran inside as I got out my car and into his.

"What did you go inside for?" I asked him as he got back in the car.

"I had to grab something." He said as he opened the secret compartment under the driver's seat. He put a brown paper bag in it then closed it back. I didn't say anything. He pulled out the driveway as his phone rang. He looked at it then put it back in the cup holder.

"Aren't you going to answer that?" I asked him.

"Nah, it's these lil niggas rushing me about this work." He said as he got on the freeway.

We made it to his parents' house in record time.

"I want to come in so I can speak." I said.

"Nah baby, stay in the car. You're going to see them soon." He said. He was in and out within two minutes. Lil Chris was asleep in his arms. He buckled him up in the seat then pulled off.

“Baby, is everything okay? You acting like you’re in a hurry.” I said.

“Yes, everything is fine. Look, when we get home I’m just dropping y’all off. I gotta drop this bag off to these lil niggas. But I’ll be back soon as I can.” He said.

“Okay.” I said with sadness in my voice. I wanted to spend some alone time with my man, and hopefully work on our second child.

“Baby, cheer up. I’m not going to be gone long. I just need like thirty minutes. Then I’ll be home to you.” He said.

“Okay.” I said smiling.

When we got to the house he carried Lil Chris inside for me, kissed me on my forehead then he was out the door. I picked up Lil Chris from the sofa and carried him to his room. I took his clothes off and put his night clothes on him.

“Mommy, can I sleep with you and daddy tonight? I had a bad dream.” He said as he opened his eyes as I was walking out of his room.

“Of course baby.” I said as I walked over to his bed, picked him up, and carried him to my room.

“Where is my daddy? He’s supposed to be here protecting us like he told me he would protect me and my sister.” He said.

"He's on his way now baby boy. And he's going to protect us. He always will." I said as I pulled my son closer to me. Then I realized that Lil Chris said something about a sister, he must be having a dream about a little sister, yeah that's it he was having a dream about me giving him a little sister. I smiled thinking about having a little girl.

Daivon

I was sitting outside one of Tim's trap houses when he walked over to the car.

"So, are you ready?" He asked as he got in the driver's side.

"Yeah, took you long enough." I said with an attitude.

"My bad ma, them niggas was in there acting like they didn't know what hell they were doing. I had to handle that. So, where are we going?" He asked me.

"I was thinking we could go back to your place. Je'leese and her boo is at the apartment." I lied.

“I thought that nigga had his own house.” Tim said as he started the car up.

“He do, I don’t know what they’re doing at the apartment.” I said.

“Okay, well put yo seat belt on. You know I drive crazy.” He said as he pulled off.

Tim lived in Redford; I missed being out there with him all the time.

“Some things never change.” I said as we got out the car.

“What you talking about?” He asked with a smile. He knew what I was talking about.

“All that money you got, and you’re still living out here.” I said

“What’s wrong with living out here? And you know I like to stack my money rather than spend it.” He said as he led the way to his house door.

“There’s nothing wrong with living out here, and again some things just never change.” I said as we both laughed.

“I know something else that hasn’t changed.” He said as he opened the door.

“And what’s that?” I asked him.

"My love for you." He said as he stepped aside so I could walk in.

"You know I'll always love you." I said as I turned toward him and kissed him.

"Mhm girl." He said as he closed the door. "Come on, let's go upstairs." He said and grabbed my hand. When we got upstairs in his room I saw that he still had the picture of us that we had painted for us one year at Cedar Point. I smiled.

"I can't believe you still got this up here." I said as I looked at it.

"Where else was I going to put it? You probably threw yours away." He said.

"No I didn't. It's in my room at the apartment." I said. And it was the truth. Only mine wasn't visible. It was sitting in the back of my closet behind some boxes.

"I'm glad to hear that." He said as he walked closer to me. "Daivon, you're so damn sexy. I can't believe I let you go without fighting for you." He said as he pulled me into his arms.

"Tim, even if you would have fought for me back then I probably still would have left." I said looking into his eyes.

“What if I fought for you now?” He asked me as he kissed and sucked on my neck.

“It doesn’t seem like you’ve changed your ways. So I’d probably be putting myself in the same position as before.” I said.

“Trust me Daivon, you know if I tell you something I mean it. I’m not in the same position anymore. I’m the boss now. I got niggas working for me. I’m no longer working for other niggas. I’m on a big come up.” He said.

“Are you sure? Because I don’t want to be hurt this time around too.” I said.

“The only person who was hurt the last time was me.” He said.

“No Tim, I was hurt too. You never showed me any attention. You just fucked me, hit me off with some cash, then you was on your way out the door.” I said.

“I’m sorry baby. I know I fucked up back then. But can you give me another chance? I promise I won’t fuck up this time.” He said.

“Are you sure?” I asked him.

“Fucking right!” He said as he grabbed my head and pulled me in for a long passionate kiss. “Lay down on the bed.” He said. I turned around and got on the bed. As soon as I lay down my whole body melted away. I didn't want to move. I watched Tim as he took of his clothes. He had dark skin and the body of a God. I knew he probably still worked out. He probably still had some work out equipment in the second bed room. He never took his eyes off me as he pulled down his boxers. I was so glad I had on my freak'em dress that I bought from the mall earlier. I didn't have a bra, but I was wearing a blue thong. Tim got on the bed and placed his body on top of mine. He looked me in my eyes as he removed the dress strap from my shoulder. Once both of the straps were down, he removed the dress from my body. He slowly removed the thong too, only he did that with his mouth. I was so wet at this point. I wanted to feel him inside of me. He started to kiss down my body. When he got to my thighs he started to lick towards my pussy. He used his tongue to please me. I released a soft moan. He used his tongue to spread my lips down there and inserted his tongue deep inside of me; he blew, sucked, and licked in a steady rhythm.

"Ooooh, oh my god!" I said grinding my hips as I gripped the back of his head with one hand and the sheets with the other. He stood up and spread my legs then draped them over his shoulders and inserted his dick inside of me. I squealed in delight. He was hitting me with some long deep strokes.

"Damn girl." He said as he released my left leg and pushed it to the side then commenced to doing some long circular strokes.

"Ooooh." I screamed out in pleasure. I came four times from him just fucking me. Tim and I fucked all night long. But my mind kept going back to Gee. Once I was done fucking over Leese, Katt, Chris, and Gee's life I could and I would commit myself to Tim. But as of now I had a secret that I needed to get off my chest.

"Tim?" I asked him as I lay in his arms after another ride.

"Wassup ma?" He asked me.

"I had an abortion two days after I left you." I said as tears rolled down my face.

Jasmine

I was still tripping over my encounter with Gee earlier. Yeah, he fucked me good. But the nigga gave me six hundred dollars. What the hell was I supposed to do with six hundred dollars? He never gave me that amount; he'd usually give me stack. I was walking out the hotel thinking about what I was going to spend my money on and wasn't watching where I was going so I walked right into Dora and her cousins

"I thought you were going home?" Dora said to me with her hands on her hips.

"I wanted to treat myself so I decided to get a room here for the night." I said coming up with a quick lie.

"You's a lying bitch. How could you? I thought we were friends?" Dora asked with tears in her eyes.

"What the hell are you talking about?" I asked trying to play it off.

"I swear on my daughter's life if you don't stop trying to play us like we stupid I'm gone beat the fucking breaks off you. We saw Gee in yo fucking car earlier. We followed y'all, we watched y'all go in and watched him come out, and we also saw when my baby daddy came to get him." Ashley said.

"Okay, if I was fucking Gee what does that have to do with Dora? He didn't put a ring on her fucking finger did he? I could have sworn he put a ring on Je'leese finger. So y'all standing here checking me over a nigga with a bitch is really stupid right now." I said, and that was the last thing that came out of my mouth before Ashley slapped me.

"Bitch, I'm not Dora. I ain't gone let yo rat ass talk to me any kind of way." Ashley said daring me to say something. Hell, I was too busy holding my face to say anything.

"I thought we were friends." Dora said as tears finally fell from her eyes.

"Dora, shut up with all that crying, shit. Asia and I both told you this bitch was a snake and for you not to trust her. But yo ass didn't listen and trusted her anyway. I told yo ass you was gone learn the hard way." Ashley said.

"Look Dora, I'm sorry. But I wanted Gee since the first time I saw him at the club. You know I was too shy to approach him. You started to talk to him so I let it go. Then I seen him at the mall a few years ago and we started fucking." I said. Dora hauled off and smacked my ass. I was tired of being hit so I swung back, and that was a bad move on my part. Asia, Ashley, and Dora jumped my ass right there in front of Greektown Hotel. Where the fuck was security when you needed them?

Giovanni

When me and Je'leese got home she went straight in the kitchen and grabbed a bottle of water.

"Do you want something to eat?" I asked her.

"Are you going to cook?" She asked me.

"If I wasn't going to cook, then I wouldn't have asked."

"Well, okay."

"Go get in the shower, and I'll be up there with some food." I told her.

Before she walked up the stairs, she walked over and stood on her tippy toes in front of me. "I love you baby." She said as she kissed my lips.

"I love you too girl." I said as I grabbed her and pulled her closer to me. I grabbed her round firm ass and squeezed it.

"You better stop before you get some shit started." She said smiling.

"If I do get some shit started we both know I can finish it." I said as I kissed her.

"I know you can baby." She said as she backed away from me.

“Damn girl, I’m so glad to have you.”

“I know baby, now go in the kitchen and cook me something to eat.” She said as she laughed and walked up the stairs. Once I was sure she was up the stairs I dialed Jasmine’s number.

“Hello.” A voice answered, and it wasn’t Jasmine.

“Who is this?” I asked.

“Is this Gee?” The voice asked, and then I recognized it as Dora’s voice.

“Dora? What are you doing with Jasmine phone?” I asked her.

“Yo lil girlfriend just got her ass beat. You and yo lil fiancée better watch out.” She said hanging up the phone. I looked at my phone wondering what the hell was going on.

Once I was done with Je’leese fries I put them on a tray along with another bottle of water and walked up the stairs to the room. When I walked in the door, Je’leese was sitting on the bed with only a towel wrapped around her body looking at the news.

“That girl Jasmine is in the hospital.” She said looking at me.

"What?" I asked her looking at the TV. I just shook my head as I gave her the tray.

"Thank you."

"Your welcome. I'm about to get in the shower." I said.

"Okay."

I was in the shower thinking about Jasmine and wondering if she really did get her ass beat. I wondered if she'd told Dora that we were fucking. I was so caught up in my thoughts, I never noticed Je'leese get in the shower with me until she wrapped her arms around my chest.

"What's wrong?" She asked me.

"Nothing, why you asking that?" I asked her as I turned to face her.

"Giovanni, I know when something is on your mind baby." She said.

"I'm just ready to leave this city, that's all." I said as she stepped back a little so she could look into my eyes.

"Is this about Jasmine?" She asked.

"What? No."

"Giovanni, don't stand here and lie to my face, I know you're thinking about her." She said.

"Alright, I am. But it's not what you think. It's just maybe she got her ass beat because of me." I said as the water splashed over both of our bodies.

"Because of you? What do you mean?" She asked me.

"I was fucking her and her best friend." I said not looking into her eyes; she didn't say anything for a long minute.

"Giovanni, you act like you forced either one of them to fuck you. I know for a fact a female will not turn you down. So don't feel get to feeling guilty that one of them fucked over the other. And they were supposed to be friends. I'm glad Katt or Dai aren't like that." She said. I didn't say anything because Daivon was like that. She was a nasty, sneaky hoe. "Giovanni, stop worrying about them and think about me, about us, and our future together. Okay?" She said.

"Okay." I said as I put my hands on her breast. I leaned in closer to her as I started to kiss her neck. I went up to her ears and took her earlobe gently between my teeth lightly nibbling on it before passionately kissing her lips. She wrapped her arms around my neck and brought my face to hers. She gave me a long, slow, loving kiss. I reached down and brought her leg up to my hip. My wet hands rubbing her thigh to the back of her knee then back again. I squeezed her ass; she let out a little moan. I broke the kiss first. I stepped back and took a long look at her, my eyes started with her feet and traveled slowly up to her body, pausing on her face, then coming to rest on her breast, which were glistening with droplets of water. I reached out and cupped the right one. I bent my head to take the nipple in my mouth. I licked and sucked on the right one then the left one. At the same time she reached down and took my dick in her hand giving it a gentle squeeze. Once her hand touched my dick it woke all the way up, growing in her hand. She took a step back then got on her knees. She licked the head of my dick, and used her mouth to caress it. She then stopped and using her tongue she licked the entire length of the shaft, up and down. I moaned and grabbed her head. She took me in her mouth and started rocking back and forth tightening the pressure of her mouth. I was fighting to hold back the nut that was sure to come any second.

She stopped at the tip. Placing her mouth over the head, she brought it down to the very base, and began sucking barely bringing her lips to the tip. That's when I shot a load deep into her throat. She swallowed and smiled up at me. I helped her up so I could kiss her. I picked her up and put her high in the air against the wall so that I could be eye level with her pussy. She wrapped her legs around my neck, so I used one of my hands to spread her lips and stuck my tongue as far inside as it could go. I gave her a few strokes with my tongue then brought my mouth down upon her mound. I took the tip of my tongue and rubbed it back and forth across her clit. I stopped and gently took the little nub and sucked at it. At the same time I used my free hand to stick one of my fingers inside of her. So while I was sucking on her I was also fucking her with my finger. She could barely contain herself. Her legs were shaking on my shoulders and she was moaning deeply not able to stand it any longer. She came all over my face. I put her down and she grabbed my arm as if she was about to fall. I grabbed her by her waist and turned her around so her back was facing me. I bent her over and she put her hands on the walls of the shower. I slowly put my eleven inches inside of her and she squealed in delight as I began to move around inside of her with amazing speed.

"Baby, this pussy is so hot." I said as I stoked inside her.

"Oohhh, I'm about to cum daddy!" She yelled out over the running water.

"Cum for me." I said as her body started to shake. Her legs looked as if they were going to give out on her, I smiled. The water that splashed on us as I stroked in and out of her felt so damn good. This wasn't my first time fucking her in the shower, but this time was so much better than last time. We both were breathing heavily after that episode in the bathroom. We dried ourselves off then went into the bedroom and did the same thing until four in the morning. After making love to her all night she was tired and worn out.

"Baby, me and Chris have something planned for you and Katt." I said to her.

“What is it?” She asked in a groggy voice.

“It’s a surprise. So just be prepared. Okay?” I said.

“Okay.” She said as she closed her eyes and fell asleep.

Jasmine

I was laying in the hospital bed thinking of all the wrongs I'd done in my life. It'd been three days since I got jumped by Dora, Ashley, and Asia. I was glad Brandy was at the hospital with me; I was so bored and needed some company. She found out what happened threw the news. After them hoes made sure I wasn't getting back up they ran. Luckily for me, a news team was riding down the street and saw me lying on the ground. I told everybody I didn't know who did it, simply because it was dark and I couldn't really see. But I didn't do it to save those hoes; I was out to get revenge when it came to Dora, Ashley, and Asia.

"So, the doctor said that everything should be fine with you before the weekend. Do you still want to go to Summer Jams and River Days?" Brandy asked me.

"I'm sorry Bran, I forgot to get the Summer Jams tickets." I said.

"Don't worry about it, I got the tickets. And we're sitting front row." Brandy said smiling.

"How did you get tickets?" I asked her sitting up.

"Girl, James gave me a stack last night. He said he hit like four licks." She said.

"That nigga had a come up huh?" I said.

“Girl, I said the same thing. I want to know what kind of lick it was. He gave all his sons a stack too. I was sitting there shocked as hell. You know that nigga so fucking stingy with his money. But I don’t think he gave his other baby mamas shit.” She said.

“They don’t deserve it. They don’t take care of their kids. Ain’t them boys always with you? And plus you have his back no matter what, that’s why his ass gave you some money.” I said.

“Well shit, that nigga need to give me more than what he did give me.” She said as we both laughed.

“Girl, yo ass is crazy.” I said.

“I’m serious, but how are you feeling?”

“I’m fine, just ready for payback.” I said. “Shit” I said in my head forgetting I told Brandy I didn’t know who jumped me either.

“So, you know who did it?” She asked.

“Yeah, it was that bitch Dora, and her cousins Ashley and Asia.” I said.

“What the hell? I thought Dora was your friend.” She said.

“Yeah, I thought so too. It was over Gee, you know I told you he stopped fucking with her and came knocking on my door saying he always wanted me in what not.” I lied

"Girl, that shit is crazy. But you know me and Candice got your back." She said.

"Yeah I know, but I can't ask y'all to get involved with my mess." I said.

"You're my cousin. You don't have to ask me." Brandy said. For the next two hours we sat there thinking about ways we could get payback on Dora, Asia, and Ashley.

Je'leese

The next morning I woke up tired and was in pain. My head was killing me, and my stomach was hurting worse than ever, it felt as if I was going to throw up the fries I ate the night before. I sat up and looked at Giovanni. He was still knocked out. I got out the bed and walked into the bathroom. I looked into the mirror and noticed that I was getting bigger. After I was done in the bathroom I walked back into the room. I put on Giovanni's shirt and boxers, and my house shoes and walked out the room. I went downstairs to the kitchen so I could cook breakfast. I was craving some pancakes and sausages. When I got in the kitchen I went to the fridge and got the sausages and the pancake mix out and sat them on the counter.

When I had the food on the stove Giovanni walked up behind me and placed his arms around me.

"When did you get up?" I asked him.

"Um, about ten minutes ago. Chris called me." He said.

"What was Chris calling about this early in the morning?"

"Somebody hit four of our shops." He said.

"Damn, do y'all know who did it?" I asked.

"He said that niggas know who did it. But they're not going to get him until the sun goes down."

"So that means I'm going to be home by myself tonight huh?" I asked him.

"For like an hour. But we do need to handle something in a lil bit." He said putting his chin on my shoulder.

"Like what?" I asked him.

"Don't worry. Just know it's a surprise for you and Katt." He said.

"I don't like surprises Giovanni" I said turning around to face him.

"Well you know I don't care. It's still a surprise no matter what you say." He said as he smiled. "Now go upstairs and find you something nice to wear on Thursday, and if you can't find anything to wear you and Katt go shopping." He said.

"But, I was cooking breakfast." I said.

"Leesy, I'm going to cook breakfast, just go do what I asked you to do." He said as he grabbed me and pulled me closer to him.

"I also wanted you to get in the shower with me." I said as I wrapped my arms around his waist.

"Baby, if I get in that shower with you we're going to be running late. And I told you I got some things to handle." He said.

"Fine." I said as I pouted.

"Don't pout, we'll get in the shower later." He said as he kissed my lips.

"Fine." I smiled at him and kissed him again then walked out of the kitchen and up the stairs. I went straight in the closet and looked at all the clothes that belonged to me in there. I didn't see anything I wanted to wear, maybe I did. But I still wanted to go shopping. I walked out the closet and over to the bed. I picked up my phone and dialed Katt's number.

"Hello." She answered after the third ring.

"What you doing girl?" I asked her.

"Sitting in this damn bed irritated."

"For what? What happened?"

"Because them dumb asses at work told me I was on the schedule today, I get down there and they tell me I didn't have to work." She said.

"Girl, they be fucking up. That's why I had to stop working there and get a job at the mall." I said.

"Hmp, y'all still hiring?" She asked.

"I don't even know. Most likely we are. But did Chris tell you anything about a surprise?" I asked her.

"Yeah, he told me that he and Gee had a surprise for me and you on Thursday." She said.

"Do you have anything to wear?" I asked her.

"Nope, I looked this morning when I came back from that dumb ass place." She said.

"I'm looking right now. I say we might as well go to the mall, because if I haven't found anything to wear yet I know I'm not going to find anything at all." I said laughing.

"Girl, you know I can never turn down a trip to the mall." She said as she laughed too.

"I know you can't. So do you want me to come get you, or are you going to come get me?" I asked her.

"You can come get me. Chris went to get my car detailed and I don't feel like driving his Mustang." She said.

"Okay, I'll be there soon." I said.

"Alright." She said as we hung up the phone. I walked into the bathroom, turned the shower on, then walked over to the sink so I could put my hair in a ponytail. Then I got in the shower.

When I got out the shower, I wrapped the towel around my body and walked over to the sink.

"Damn baby, you're getting thick." Giovanni said as he walked up behind me.

"I've been thick." I said laughing.

"Well you're getting thicker." He said as he wrapped his arms around me.

"Thicker than a snicker. But I just said the same thing." I said as we both laughed.

"You know I love the smell of that body wash." He said as he put his face in my neck and kissed and licked on it.

"Giovanni, stop while you're ahead. I need to go to the mall and you got stuff that you need to handle." I said, because I knew if he kept at it we were going to be indulging in another session.

"I know, but I'm going to finish this tonight when I get home." He said as he kissed me on my cheek.

"Is the food finished?" I asked him.

"Yeah, it's on the table waiting for us." He said.

"So, we're eating at the table?" I asked him.

"Yes ma'am." He said as he walked out the bathroom. I was going to flat iron my hair, but thought better of it. I kept the ponytail in and walked out the bathroom. Giovanni was sitting on the bed.

"Are you going to eat in that?" He asked me as he licked his lips. I had actually forgotten I had the towel wrapped around my body.

"No, I'm going to put on this robe." I said as I grabbed my light blue robe that was hanging inside the closet.

"I'd much rather you wear that towel." He said as I put the robe on.

"I know you would." I said as we both smiled and walked out the room and down the stairs. When we got into the kitchen, Giovanni had both of our plates on the table along with some orange juice.

"This looks and smells so good. Thank you." I said as we sat down.

"Your welcome." He said.

After we got done eating we both went upstairs. I put on some clothes while Giovanni was in the shower. I was so tempted to go get in the shower and join him, but I knew I had to go get Katt. By the time he got out the shower I was gone. When I got to Chris' house, I called Katt and she came right out the door.

"Took yo ass long enough," she said as she got into my car.

"Girl, when I called you I still had to get in the shower, and eat breakfast." I said as she put her seat belt on.

"What do you think these fools got planned for Thursday?" She asked me.

"I don't know. But whatever it is, I hope it's good." I said as I pulled off. "Where is my god son?" I asked her.

"He's with his father, you know he wants to hang with the boys instead of coming to the mall with me and you." She said.

"I miss his bad self." I said as I got on I75 heading towards Fairlane Mall.

"He misses you too. He just asked about you and Gee yesterday. Talking about mommy, where has my nanny and Parian been?" She said while laughing.

"I'm gone have to come get him this weekend." I said as Katt looked at me.

"Leese, girl you're getting big. What have you been eating?" She asked me.

"Nothing, I haven't been able to keep any food down." I said.

"Did you go to the doctors yet?" She asked me.

"No, I go this Friday that was the only day available." I said.

"Have you been throwing up?" She asked me.

"Yeah." I said.

"Girl, you're pregnant." She said. I laughed.

"My ass ain't pregnant. Shit if Giovanni got anybody pregnant it's one of his many hoes." I said still laughing.

"Girl bye, I said the same thing with Lil Chris. I'm sure you remember." She said as I turned into the mall parking lot.

"I'm not trying to hear that pregnant stuff right now. I'll just prove you wrong Friday at this appointment." I said.

"And I'll be there just to prove you wrong." She said.

"Okay."

Chris

Lil Chris and I were in the car riding to pick Gee up so we could go handle the stuff that needed to be handled for Thursday. I was just getting off the freeway when my cell phone rang. It was Ashley.

"Hello." I answered. I turned the music up because I knew she was gone say some stupid shit.

"When can I see my daughter?" She asked me with hella noise in her background.

"If she goes to River Days Thursday you can see her there. If not I'll just meet you somewhere." I said.

"Why can't you just bring her to my crib?" She asked.

"Because she's not coming back over there," I stated.

"Well can you meet me somewhere right now?"

"Look Ashley I'm busy right now and I'll be busy tomorrow also. But if you want to see her I told you I'm thinking about letting her go to River Days. If she do, I'll have my parents meet you somewhere there, if not, you gone have to wait until I'm not busy." I said hanging up the phone. As soon as I put it in the cup holder, it rang again. This time it was my nigga Gee.

"Hello."

"Where you at?" He asked me.

"Pulling up, come outside."

"Fasho." He said as I hung up the phone. As I pulled up in his driveway, Gee was coming outside. He got in the car and I turned down the music.

"Wassup Lil Chris?" He said.

"Hey Parian, I'm hanging with you and my daddy today." Lil Chris said.

"I see, you hanging with the big dogs huh?" Gee said laughing.

"Yes sir." Lil Chris said.

"Has anyone said anything else?" Gee asked me, I turned the music up some so Lil Chris wouldn't hear this conversation either, but he was so busy playing his DSI that he wasn't paying me and Gee any attention.

"Nope. The only thing niggas is saying is Lil James the one that did it." I said.

"The one that lives out there in Southwest?"

"The very same." I said.

"That nigga must not want to see his kids grow up." He said shaking his head.

“Hell no he don’t, but he gone learn his lesson tonight.”

After we made sure everything was set for tomorrow, I dropped Lil Chris off at my parents’ house then we headed to the four stash houses that were hit.

“Man, that nigga had to be working with somebody.” I said.

“Ain’t no nigga gone take the same amount of money from four different houses by his self.” Gee said.

“He had to be working with somebody from the inside.” I said.

“Man. The shit is crazy. I say we move all the money to the girls’ apartment in Je’leese room. I got a safe in there, nobody but Je’leese knows it’s in there. But she won’t go in there unless I tell her to.” He said.

“Alright, I’m gone call the workers and tell them to pack all the money up. We gone pick it up after we finish with James ass.” I said.

“Fasho.” He said.

Katherine

Me and Je'leese were in the mall until it got ready to close. We went in there looking for one outfit and came out with more than one. When she dropped me off at home, Christopher and Lil Chris were still out. I called Christopher's phone three times and each time it went straight to voicemail. As I was dialing his number the fourth time, he was calling my phone.

"Hello." I said making sure he knew I had an attitude.

"What's up baby, did you call?" He asked me.

"No Christopher, I just dialed your number three times." I said rolling my eyes.

"What's wrong with you?" He asked.

"Nothing, where are you and Lil Chris at?"

"There is something wrong with you. But he's at my parents' house. After he rode around with me and his Parian I took him over there so I could handle my business." He said.

"What time are you coming home?" I wanted to know.

"I don't know. I'll try to be there before eleven."

"Yeah okay."

"I'm serious baby."

"I hear you."

"I love you." He said.

"I love you too." I said hanging up the phone. Once I got off the phone with him I took a bubble bath.

When I got out the bath tub it was going on eleven. I knew Christopher's ass wasn't going to be home until after one. I went downstairs to fix me something to snack on before I went to bed. I fixed me a grilled cheese. As soon as I was done fixing my sandwich, the house phone rang. I walked into the living room with my plate in my hand.

"Hello." I answered.

"Is Chris home?" A female asked.

"No he's not. Who is this?" I asked. I couldn't believe Chris had bitches calling the house phone at this time of night for him.

"My name is Ashley, when Chris gets home can you have him call me. Or can you just tell him I want to see my daughter." The girl said.

"Um, what do you mean you want your daughter?" I asked her.

"My daughter is with Chris, he's had her for a few weeks now, and I miss her." Ashley said.

"I'm confused, why would Christopher have your daughter?" I asked her.

"He has her because he's her father." Ashley said.

"Is this some sort of joke?" I asked her.

"Do this sound like a joke? My daughter name is Christina. And she's four years old." Ashley said.

"And you say Christopher is your baby's father?" I asked her making sure I heard right.

"Yeah, I thought he would have told you once he took her from my house. But I guess not. When you talk to him, tell him I want to see my daughter." She said.

"I sure will tell him." I said as I hung up the phone. I sat down on the sofa. I didn't even want to eat anymore; my head was in over drive thinking about this. I couldn't believe some girl called my phone telling me she had a child by Chris. Maybe this was some sort of joke. Maybe it's one of his many hoes calling the phone trying to get his attention. Yeah, that's it! I said as I got up from the sofa and walked up the stairs and into my room still thinking about that call. I knew it was going to be hard for me to get to sleep with that on my brain.

Je'leese

I was still up for some strange reason worrying about Giovanni. I hadn't spoken to him since earlier. That was around nine and here it was going on three in the morning. I didn't know what he was out there doing; his phone was going straight to voicemail and it was really making me mad. I sat in the bed wondering was he out cheating on me, or was he somewhere hurt, or was he locked up in jail. I didn't know what to think until I heard the front door open and close then somebody walking up the stairs. I gave a sigh of relief when Giovanni walked into the room. I got out the bed and ran to him and hugged him.

"What's wrong?" He asked me.

"I thought something happened to you." I said as I buried my face in his shirt and tears rolled down my face.

"I'm okay baby. Ain't nothing gone happen to me." He said as he pulled me away from him. I looked up into his eyes and smiled as he wiped the tears away.

"I love you Giovanni." I said.

"I love you more baby." He said as he pulled me in for a kiss.

"I swear, if you ever scare me like that again, I will make something happen to you." I said.

"As long as it has something to do with pleasure I'm cool with it." He said as I smiled.

"You're not funny." I said and playfully punched him in his chest.

"I'm glad you were worried about me." He said.

"I'm always worried about you baby." I said.

"And that's why I love you." He said.

"Baby, what's that on your shoes?" I asked him as I looked down at his all white Air Force Ones.

"Don't worry about that baby, it's nothing." He said.

"Giovanni, is that blood?" I asked him.

"Baby. Please don't worry about this." He said again.

"Don't worry about it Giovanni? You come in this house at three in the morning with blood on your shoes and you're going to tell me not to worry about it?" I asked him as he walked into our closet. I followed him.

"Baby, it's nothing. You know what goes on in the streets stays in the streets, so please leave it alone." He said as he grabbed him some night clothes and walked past me. I went and got in the bed and turned off the lamp that was on my night stand. I was trying to fall asleep, but I knew it was going to be damn near impossible without

Giovanni holding me. That's one thing I didn't like about me being mad at him or him being mad at me, because I would have to fall asleep without him holding me. Even when I was staying at the apartment with Katt and Dai he would spend the night with me most nights, or I would spend the night with him. Overall, he usually held me at night. But tonight I didn't want him touching me.

Jasmine

It was Thursday morning and I was finally being released from the hospital. I was so happy to be going home. Brandy and Candice came to pick me up. The first thing I wanted to do was go home so I could have a proper meal then some rest so I could be energized for the night. But I knew I had to go to Sprint to get me another phone since Dora's ass took my other one. It was the first night of River Days and I wanted to have some fun before I got my payback with Dora, Ashley, and Asia.

"How are you feeling girl?" Candice asked me as I got in the backseat of Brandy's car.

"I just need to eat me some real food then sleep in my own bed, then I'll be good." I said as Brandy pulled off.

“Are we still going out tonight?” Brandy asked me.

“Girl yes, this little bruise under my eye can be covered with some makeup. Besides I wouldn’t miss tonight for nothing in the world. It’s gone be some fine niggas out there tonight like it is every year.

“Have you talked to Gee?” Brandy asked me.

“Girl no. But I know him and his homie Chris always go to River Days on the first day. So I’ll see him tonight.” I said.

“Girl, I can’t wait.” Candice said.

After we went to Sprint we went to my house. They walked in with me to make sure Dora, Ashley, and Asia weren’t hiding in my closet. I told them that it wasn’t necessary, but they said, even though I was feeling better and all, I was still in no condition to fight them hoes again right now. But when I had my strength back, them hoes had it coming. I didn’t give a damn if I could fight or not I was fighting them hoes.

“Are you going to be okay here for a couple hours?” Brandy asked me.

“Yeah girl. I’m about to take me a nice warm bubble bath, and then a nap. I’ll give you my extra key in case I’m still sleep when y’all are on the way.” I said as I walked over to the entertainment system and grabbed the spare key that was under my bible.

"Okay girl, I'll call you at like five." Brandy said.

"Alright." I said as I walked her and Candice to the door. Once they were in the car, I closed the door, locked it, and walked to my room. I was so happy to be home. I walked in the bathroom and ran me some water in the tub. I put some bubbles in the water then lit some candles. I then walked into my room, grabbed my new phone off the dresser, and dialed Gee's number.

"Hello." He answered.

"Hey stranger." I said.

"Who is this?"

"Jasmine."

"Oh, wassup Jas? How you doing?" He asked me as he turned the music down in his back ground.

"I'm good. You couldn't come see me huh?" I asked him as I started to take my clothes off.

"You know it's not like that. I've been taking care of some business. But are you doing any better?" He asked me.

"Yeah, I'm straight. Them weak bitches ain't stopping shit this way." I said.

"I hear that. What you got up for the day?" He asked me.

"Nothing right now, I'm about to take a bubble bath, then a nap. My cousin is taking me to River Days later. Are you going?" I asked him.

"Yeah I'll be down there later with the Mrs. But look, I got some business that I'm trying to handle right now. I'll talk to you later." He said.

"Okay." I said as we hung up the phone. I was glad to hear his voice. I just hoped he'd be in my bed tonight.

Giovanni

Me and Chris were in the car on our way to the Coleman A Young Center so we could marry Je'leese and Katt.

"Katt was acting weird as hell last night man." Chris said as I looked through my phone and started deleting numbers.

"Je'leese got mad. I had that fool blood on my shoes, she saw it." I said shaking my head.

"When are you going to tell her about Daivon?" Chris asked me.

"I don't know, maybe I'll tell her tomorrow after Summer Jams." I said.

"Shit, I was thinking about telling Katt about Christina tonight at the room." Chris said.

"You sure you're ready for that? Because you know she might try to kill you in there." I said laughing.

"Y'all room right next to ours, if you hear us going at it come in and check on us. I don't want to die right now. And I know she's going to be extra mad because she's been wanting another kid for the longest, and I've been hiding this kid for two years, almost three." Chris said.

“Man, how can you hide something that big for that long? You must have been hitting that bitch Ashley off with some serious loot.” I said laughing.

“Man, you don’t even know the half of it. That bitch was trying to take me for all the money I had. But my pops is supposed to bring Lil Chris and Christina to the ceremony.” Chris said.

“Isn’t Katt going to notice that there’s a little girl there that looks just like her son and her fiancée?” I asked him.

“Yeah she’s going to notice, but she won’t say anything until after all the excitement is over.” He said laughing.

“True.” I said as my cell phone rung. I looked down at the screen and it was Daivon. I answered it.

“I guess I need to start speaking in Spanish for you to understand me since English isn’t working. Didn’t I tell yo ass not to call me anymore?” I asked her.

“Damn, I see your attitude hasn’t changed.” She said.

“Bitch look, I don’t have time to put up with your bullshit, what the fuck do you want?” I asked her.

“Come over tonight.” She said.

“Nah, I got some shit to handle.” I said.

"And what's that? Planning your wedding?" She asked laughing.

"Bye Daivon." I said.

"Alright, then come over in the morning we need to talk about your plans." She said.

"And what plans might that be?" I asked her.

"Don't worry about it. Just be at the apartment in the morning." She said.

"And if I don't?" I asked her.

"Come on na, you can't think I only had one copy of those photos. Just because you took my phone don't mean I didn't have more copies. Now it's either you be over here or I send them to Je'leese and Katt." She said. I didn't even reply to her ass, I just hung up the phone.

"Fuck man!" I screamed hitting the dash board.

"What's going on man?" Chris asked me.

"That bitch Daivon got another copy of them pictures. She said if I don't come over to the apartment tomorrow she's going to send them to Leesy and Katt." I said shaking my head.

"Man that bitch done lost her mind." Chris said.

"Tell me about it. But she about to find that mother-fucker tomorrow." I said.

When we got to the center Chris' father Charles was there along with Lil Chris and Christina.

"Hey pops." Chris said as Charles shook both of our hands.

"How are y'all doing?" He asked us.

"We're doing fine. Just ready to marry these crazy women we have." I said.

"Are y'all sure about this? Y'all know after this y'all have to be fully committed to them and just them." Charles said.

"We're ready pops. Katherine and Je'leese are the only women we want to be with." Chris said.

"What about Ashley and Daivon?" He asked looking from Chris to me.

"Sir, what happened between me and Daivon was a mistake. I messed with her twice while I was drunk. One of those nights she messed around with me and Chris, the second night was a huge mistake, and the third time was because she was black-mailing me. But I'm going to tell Je'leese about it this weekend." I said.

"Good, and what are you going to do about Ashley and your daughter?" He asked turning his attention to Chris.

"I'm going to tell Katt about it tonight." Chris said.

"Are you sure about that?" Charles asked.

"Yes I am. She deserves to know, and I want to tell her before Ashley tries to tell her again." Chris said.

"Okay, well we're taking the kids to Chuckie Cheese and the movies after this. I know you said you don't want the kids at River Days. Are y'all going?" Charles asked us.

"Yeah we're going later." Chris said.

Katherine

I was in the car with Je'leese and Chris' mother Renee, who was driving and we were headed downtown. My mind was still on that news from last night. Then I thought back to what Lil Chris said the night we picked him up from his grandparent's house. I thought he was just having a dream about a little sister, but he must been talking about his real little sister that his father has been hiding from me. I didn't tell Je'leese or Renee because I didn't know what to say. I had a feeling Renee already knew but wasn't going to say anything until Chris said something. That's just how mothers are.

"Katt, what's wrong honey?" Renee asked me.

"Nothing, I just have a lot on my mind." I said as we turned into the parking lot for the Coleman A Young Center.

"Is everything okay?" Je'leese asked me.

"Yes, everything is fine. What are we doing here?" I asked Renee.

"We're meeting the guys here." Renee said. We got out the car and Renee made sure both my and Je'leese's hair was up to par. We both had on white dresses, with some white Red bottom heels.

"Both of y'all look so beautiful." Renee said.

"Thanks mama." Both Je'leese and I said at the same time.

"Come on." She said as she led the way into the center. When we got in there we walked towards a dressing room.

"What are we doing in here?" I asked her.

"This is where you two will sit until the wedding starts." She said smiling.

"What wedding?" I asked. Je'leese looked at me. Then I thought about it.

"Chris and Giovanni brought both of you here so they could marry you." Renee said.

"Oh my god!" Je'leese said as she smiled. But I wasn't so happy.

"Katt, why don't you look happy?" Je'leese asked me.

"I am happy." I said as I put on a fake smile.

"I'll go let the guys know we're here." Renee said as she walked out the dressing room.

"Katt, what's wrong?" Je'leese asked me as soon as Renee closed the door.

“I think Christopher has another child.” I said as some tears escaped my eyes.

“What? Why do you think that?” She asked me as I sat down on the sofa.

“Because, some girl named Ashley called me last night and asked to speak to Chris. Chris wasn’t home and I told her that. So she asked me to pass a message along to him saying she wanted to see her daughter. I asked her why Chris would have her daughter and she told me Chris was the father of her four-year-old daughter Christina.” I said as the tears fell faster and faster.

“Aw, best friend. Stop crying.” Je’leese said as she sat next to me and rubbed my back.

“Leese, I don’t know what to do.” I said as I wiped the tears from my eyes.

“Do you love Chris?” She asked me.

“Yes I love Chris.” I said.

“Do you want to spend the rest of your life with him?” She asked me.

“Of course I want to.” I said.

“Then you know what you need to do. Go out there and marry the man you love.” She said.

Daivon

Gee may have hung up on me, but I knew he was going to come in the morning. I've been trying to get in touch with his bitch all day. She wasn't answering her phone and neither was Katt. I wondered what those hoes were up to. I sat on the bed waiting on Tim to come get me so we could go to River Days where I was sure to run into Katt, Chris, Leese, and Gee. I was about to get out the bed so I could put my hair in a ponytail when my cell phone rang. I looked at the screen and it was Je'leese.

"Hello." I answered.

"What's up? My bad I didn't answer the phone earlier. I was in the car with Katt and Chris' mama and didn't hear it ringing." She said.

"It's cool. What are y'all up to?" I asked her.

"Meeting up with Chris and Giovanni right now." She said.

"What do y'all got up? And are y'all going to River Days?" I asked her.

"I don't know, and most likely we'll be there. You know we don't miss a year of it." She said as she laughed.

"Well, hopefully Tim and I see y'all there." I said.

"So, are y'all back together?" She asked me.

"Something like that. He wants me to move in with him. I know you and Katt have moved in with Gee and Chris so what are we going to do about the apartment?" I asked her. But I really didn't care what happened to it.

"Um, I mean we can still keep it in case I get mad at Giovanni or you and Katt get mad at Chris or Tim. You know we don't like to be around them." She said.

"Well that can work. But what about the bills?" I asked her.

"Girl, you know Chris and Giovanni always pay the bills. They can continue to pay them." She said as we both laughed.

"Well, that sounds like a plan to me." I said.

"But look, I gotta go. Chris mama needs to talk to me. I'll see you later." She said.

"Okay." I said hanging up the phone. As soon as I hung up the phone somebody knocked on my door. I walked out my room and walked into the living room to answer the door.

"Who is it?" I yelled out.

"It's me ma!" Tim said from the other side of the door. When I opened the door he was standing there with some flowers in his hand smiling a smile that made my heart fluttered.

“Are those for me?” I asked him as he walked past me and into the house. I closed the door and turned around to face him.

“Yeah ma.” He said as he kissed my lips. I was glad he wasn’t mad or upset about the secret I told him the other night. After I told him about the abortion he didn’t say anything to me. He just pulled me closer and held me the entire night as I cried. I had a feeling he was crying too, but I never looked to see.

Katherine

An hour later I finally became Mrs. Christopher James Butler Sr., and Je'leese became Mrs. Giovanni Robert Smith. After the ceremony we went out to eat at Benihana's. Charles and Renee took Lil Chris and who I'm guessing was Christina to Chuckie Cheese and the movies. After we went out to eat we went to the double room suite we had at Greektown. I was sitting on the bed while Christopher was pouring some champagne into two glasses.

"Why are you so quiet?" Christopher asked me as he handed me one of the glasses. I took a sip of it then placed it on the table next to the bed.

"Is she the reason you didn't want to give me another child?" I asked him in a low tone.

"Huh, what are you talking about?" He asked me. I stood up.

"Christopher, please don't stand here play stupid. Is she the reason you didn't want to give me another child because you already had one?" I asked him as the tears fell from my eyes.

"How do you know?" He asked me.

"Your baby mother called the house last night saying she wanted to see her daughter." I said. He put his glass down and walked towards me. He reached his hand out and tried to grab mine. But I yanked it away from him.

"Don't touch me." I said.

"Katherine, it's not what you think." He said.

"Not what I think? Christopher you have a daughter, a daughter who is four years old and it's not what I think? Then what is it? Please tell me!" I yelled.

"Katherine calm down." He said.

I sat down on the bed and put my head in my hands.

"Katt, will you please listen to me?" He asked me.

I didn't even know what to say.

He sat next to me. "I didn't even know Ashley had a baby until two years ago. She told me she had a little girl. I asked her who the father was and she told me I was the father. I didn't believe her so I got a DNA test, the test came back that I was the father." He said.

I raised my head up and looked at him. "And I should have known two years ago when you found out." I said as more tears streamed down my face. I didn't even bother to wipe them.

"I'm sorry Katt. I was going to tell you before we went to River Days. I wanted you to meet her." He said.

"Was that her today?" I asked him. But I already knew the answer.

"Yes." He said. I knew that was her. She looked just like both Chris and Lil Chris. "Can you please forgive me?" He asked me as he grabbed one of my hands.

"I don't know Christopher. Do you know how I feel right now?" I asked.

"Baby, I know you're hurt and feeling betrayed. But I never meant for you to get hurt. I really am sorry! But believe me I wanted to tell you. I just didn't know how." Christopher said.

"I can forgive you Christopher. But I will never forget this." I said as I got up and walked into the bathroom.

Je'leese

Me and Giovanni were just getting out the shower after several sessions of love making.

"Baby?" I asked him as we sat on the bed in our robes.

"Yes?" He said as he went over to our bags that were on the table.

"Did you know about Chris having a daughter?" I asked him already knowing the answer before he said it.

"Yeah, but I promised him I wouldn't say anything until he told Katt." He said.

"But you could have told me." I said.

"Leesy, if I would have told you then you would have told Katt." He said as he pulled out a pair of black True Religion shorts, and a black True Religion shirt.

"Do you have any children out there I don't know about?" I asked him.

"No baby, that's something you don't need to worry about. I used condoms, and if a hoe did come to me saying she was pregnant I'd tell her to get an abortion." He said.

"What about me? Would you tell me to get an abortion?" I asked him.

"Hell no girl. You are the only woman I want to have my child." He said as he walked over to me. I smiled.

"Speaking of babies, Katt thinks I'm pregnant." I said to him.

"Are you?" He asked me.

"No I'm not. But I do have a doctor's appointment tomorrow." I said.

"Well if you are then you know I'm going to take care of mine." He said.

"I know you will." I said smiling.

"I love you Mrs. Smith. You are the only woman I will ever love besides my mother and my daughters, when you give me some." He said as I pulled his face toward me for a kiss.

"I love you more Mr. Smith. I don't know what I would do if I didn't have you in my life." I said.

After we had our clothes on we went next door to Katt and Chris' room. When they opened the door and I walked, I wanted to walk right back out. I knew Katt and Chris had the conversation about Chris' child and I knew that Katt was upset.

"Are you guys okay?" I asked them.

“We’re fine. But Leese, I wanted to know if you’d christen my daughter.” Chris asked. I was caught off guard by the question.

“Um, sure.” I said as I looked over at Katt. She was wiping tears from her eyes.

“Are you guys still going to River Days?” Giovanni asked.

“Are we Katt?” Chris asked her.

“Yeah, I don’t want to be sitting in this room right now.” She said as she stood up and walked out the room. I followed behind her.

“Are you okay?” I asked her once we were in the hallway heading to the elevators.

“I don’t know Leese. This shit hurts more than anything. I was praying to God that it wasn’t his baby, and the girl was just playing on my phone. But she’s his baby.” She said as she broke down.

“So, what are you going to do?” I asked her.

“I’m going to take care of her as if she was my own.” She said.

“You’re a strong woman. I don’t know too many women like you. I don’t know how I would feel if Giovanni had a child outside of our relationship. You are so strong.” I said.

"Thanks best friend, and I mean for everything." She said as Giovanni and Chris walked up behind us.

"Are y'all ready?" Giovanni asked us.

"Yeah." I said as the elevators doors opened and we got on.

Jasmine

It was going on six and River Days was jammed packed. I was walking around with Brandy and Candice. So far I got four different numbers, and they all were paid. Three of them were drug dealers, and the other one was a wanna-be rapper. I've never heard any of his music. I got their numbers because I knew Gee was in love with Je'leese and I wasn't about to keep coming in between them.

"Look, isn't that Gee?" Brandy asked me.

"Yeah, that's him, his girl, his right hand man, and his girl best friend." I said as they walked towards the place we were standing.

"Are you going to speak?" Candice asked me.

"Nah, not while he's with his girl." I said.

"Well I'm going to speak to his ass." Brandy said.

"No Bran…" I said, but it was too late.

"Hey Gee." Brandy said. I turned my back towards them.

"Wassup?" Gee asked.

"Jasmine, aren't you going to speak?" Candice asked me. I turned around and Gee was standing in front of me holding his girl hand.

"Hey Gee." I said.

"Wassup Jas, I see you're feeling better." He said as if he didn't talk to me earlier on the phone.

"Yeah, them weak bitches couldn't hold me down." I said playing along with his little game.

"Well, it was nice seeing and talking to you again. But we need to keep walking. I'll talk to you another time." He said.

As soon as they walked away I gave Candice and Brandy the evil eye.

"What? Didn't you say you wanted that nigga in your bed tonight?" Candice asked me.

"Yeah, but that was his fiancée, I was going to text him later tonight. Not be like 'Hey Gee, I want you in my bed tonight.'" I said as Brandy and Candice started laughing.

"Girl bye." Brandy said as we started walking again.

"Whatever." I said as we stood in line to get an Elephant Ear.

"But girl, did y'all see the way his bitch looked at Candice?" Brandy asked.

"That bitch don't play no games. She's crazy as hell. I went to Northwestern with her and she fought like every four months. And it was all over Gee." Candice said.

"Isn't that Dora and her cousins?" Brandy asked. Me and Candice turned our heads to where she pointed.

Chris

"Chris, where the hell is my daughter?" Ashley asked me as she and her sister and cousin walked up to me, Katt, Gee, and Leese.

"Ashley, don't come over here with all that bullshit man." I said as I looked at Katherine, she was looking at Leese.

"Fuck that! Nigga where the fuck is my daughter?" Ashley asked.

"She's with my parents. Na Ashley gone with all that bullshit." I said.

"I'm not going no fucking where, I want my daughter." She said.

"Look, he told you that his parents have her, so get the fuck out his face." Katherine said. And I knew from then on it was going to be some shit popping off.

"Oh, so he told you huh? Was it before or after I called your house phone?" Ashley asked.

"It doesn't matter when he told me, just know he told me. And I'm not going anywhere." Katherine said.

"That's good for you." Ashley said as she smirked at me.

"Y'all thought y'all was gone get away with jumping me you no good ass bitches?" Jasmine asked as her and her friends walked up from behind Ashley and her crew.

"Aww shit." Gee said.

"Bitch, you better get the fuck on. I'm not about to deal with yo hoe ass right now." Ashley said.

"Bitch, I don't give a damn what you want. Y'all hoes jumped me and I refuse to let y'all get away with it." Jasmine said.

"Wait a minute, which one of y'all fucked with Giovanni?" Je'leese asked.

“Bitch mind ya fucking business. What you need to worry about is Gee taking care of my cousin baby.” Ashley said.

“That bitch ain’t pregnant by me and watch yo fucking mouth bitch.” Gee said to Ashley.

“And if she don’t what the fuck you gone do?” Asia asked

“You don’t want to see what’s going to happen if she don’t. And bitch I don’t know who the fuck you think you’re talking to but I’ll beat the breaks off you. And whichever one of them is your fucking cousin ain’t pregnant by Giovanni. And if she is we’ll see when the DNA test gets here.” Je’leese said as she moved closer to Ashley and her crew.

“Leese, calm down.” Katt said giving her an eye. But before anybody else could say anything Jasmine and her girls started fighting Ashley, Asia, and Dora.

“Come on man.” I said to Gee.

“Man, that shit is crazy as hell.” Gee said as we walked towards the exit.

“Are y’all leaving already?” Daivon asked us as her and some nigga walked in.

“Yeah, shit got a lil crazy back there.” Katherine said.

“Hey Tim.” Leese said.

"Wassup Leese, Katt?" The dude named Tim said.

"Tim, these are Je'leese and Katherine's fiancées Gee and Chris. Y'all this is my boyfriend Tim." She said introducing me and Gee to her nigga. Neither me nor Gee acknowledged the dude.

"Maybe we can do something tomorrow before or after Summer Jams." Daivon said smiling at Gee, and I knew she was trying to be funny.

"Alright, I'll call you later." Leese said.

"Okay." Daivon said as she and Tim walked past us.

"That was so damn rude." Leese said.

"What was?" Gee asked her.

"Not speaking to Tim." She said.

"The nigga didn't speak to us." Gee said.

"Come on man, this supposed to be our honeymoon night, let's not argue and ruin it." I said.

"Yo ass already ruined it." Katherine said a she looked at me.

"Chris is right, let's just go back to the hotel and have a nice dinner. Then we can retire to our rooms and spend some quality time with our partners." Leese said.

"Fine." Katt said.

Katherine

After dinner at Fishbone, Christopher and I were back in our room. I was sitting on the sofa and he was sitting at the table. The TV was on, but I had the volume down.

"Are we going to talk at all?" He asked me, I looked at him and rolled my eyes.

"What is there to talk about? You fucked another bitch and got her pregnant. Now y'all have a four year old daughter, and you kept this shit from me for two fucking years." I said with tears in my eyes.

"Katherine, you said you forgave me." He said.

"Yes, I did say I forgive you, but I also said I would never forget it." I said.

"Katt, baby I'm sorry. I thought if I would have told you then you would have left me and you would have taken my son with you." He said.

"Christopher, you know damn well I wouldn't keep Lil Chris from you. You kept that from me for your own selfish ass reason." I said wiping the tears from my eyes. I stood up.

"Katherine, baby please. I really am sorry." He said as he stood up. But I walked toward the bedroom door. Before I opened the door he grabbed my arm, turned me around, and pushed me against the door. He grabbed my wrist and put them above my head. He looked me in my eyes as he pushed his body against mine. Then he leaned down and kissed me on my lips. I tried to move my head at first but I quickly stopped once I felt his tongue on my bottom lip. I opened my mouth and allowed his tongue to enter my mouth. He let go of my hands and started to run his hands down my body. I moaned at his touch. He then raised one of my legs up to his waist; I wrapped my arms around his neck. He picked up my other leg and put it around his waist. He opened the door and walked through it. He had both of his hands on my ass as he walked towards the bed. I broke the kiss to look him in his eyes as tears rolled down my face. He sat me down on the bed and removed my shirt, then his, before he leaned down and kissed me again. He undid my bra without breaking the kiss.

He ran his hand along my waistband, then slowly slipped his hand into my jeans. He gently started to rub my pussy.

"Mmm." I moaned, then he took his hand out of my pants and pulled them down. Once my pants were on the floor he took off his pants and boxers and I pulled off my boy shorts. He climbed on the bed and got on top of me. He entered me with one swift motion.

"Ooh!" I yelled out in pleasure. He started to push himself deep inside of me. We traded positions after five minutes of him on top. He was now lying on his back, and I was on top of him. His hands were on my hips as I started to go up and down, faster and faster. He moaned as his eyes rolled to the back of his head. He let my hips go and grabbed my breast and started to play with my nipples. Again, we traded positions, I was now on my back again, and he was on top of me.

"Ohh God, this feels so good." I moaned loudly as he picked up a faster rhythm. He put both of my legs on his shoulder. "I'm about toooo cummmm." I yelled out.

"Cum for daddy." Christopher said as he stroked faster and faster.

"Ahhhhhh!" I yelled out as I came all over his dick. He moaned as he continued to stroke me.

"Shiitttt!" He grunted as he collapsed on me. He rested his head on my shoulder as we tried to catch our breath. I moved my fingers along his back as he kissed my neck. He lifted his body up some so he could look at me.

"I love you and I didn't mean to hurt you." He said as tears fell from his eyes and I wiped them away.

Giovanni

I was laying in the bed with Je'leese in my arms after yet another session of love making.

"Giovanni?" She asked me.

"Huh?" I asked.

"Which one of them lil hoes did you fuck?" She asked me.

"The short one." I said.

"You got a thing for short females huh?" She asked me as she climbed on top of me.

"I only have a thing for you." I said as I rubbed my hands up and down her side.

"I'm just glad Daivon finally found her somebody." She said.

"Baby, I don't want to spend our honeymoon night talking about that bitch. I want to spend it talking about us." I said.

"Fine." She said as she leaned down and kissed my lips.

"I swear baby, even though you gettin thicker you still the finest woman in this world." I said smiling.

"Thank you baby." She said as I placed her right nipple in my mouth. "Ouch." She said.

"What's wrong?" I asked her.

"It hurt when you sucked on my nipple." She said.

I looked at her, "I'm sorry."

"It's okay." She said as I pulled her face down so I could kiss her. She lifted her bottom up then she grabbed my already hard dick and placed it inside of her, she gasped as she slid down on it. I reached up and took her breast in my hands squeezing them as she began to rock back and forth slowly. Her eyes were closed as I caressed her breast.

"Ooooh, yes that feels so good." She moaned as I placed my hands on her hips and she started to slide up and down on my dick.

"Damn girl, ride this dick." I said as I placed both of my hands on each of her cheeks.

"Oh god, I'm about too cummmm!" She yelled out as I grabbed her waist again, I pulled down as I slammed upward.

"Shiiiiitttt." She yelled out as she came all over my dick. I flipped her over so that she was on her back, and I was on top. It was time for me to cum. I begin to stoke her fast. Her moans were soon muffled as I brought my face down to kiss her.

"I'm about to cum." I said as I exploded inside of her.

"I love you Je'leese Smith." I said, but she didn't answer. Her eyes were closed. She was knocked out cold. I smiled as I got out the bed to take a shower, before I walked out the room and into the bathroom my cell phone rang. I grabbed it from my shorts then walked into the bathroom.

"Hello." I answered.

"Don't you sound sexy?" Daivon said.

"Hoe, what the fuck do you want?" I asked her.

"Are you still coming over in the morning" She asked me as I turned the shower on.

"Yeah." I said.

"Okay, I can't wait to see you." She said.

I hung up the phone, deleted the call from my call log, and turned the phone off before I got in the shower.

Jasmine

It was seven in the morning and me, Brandy, and Candice were being released from the jail house.

"Man, that shit was so crazy." Brandy said as we walked towards the Marriott parking lot.

"Tell me about it. Y'all don't know how bad my damn body hurts." I said. Then we all burst out laughing.

"Did y'all see Asia face after I was done beating that ass?" Candice asked us.

"Candice, I thought yo ass was too stuck up to fight anybody." I said as we crossed the street.

"Shit, don't sleep on my girl Candice. She ah beast with them hands." Brandy said.

When we got to Brandy's car I got in the back, Brandy got in the driver's seat and Candice got in the passenger side. As soon as Brandy started the car up my mind went back to earlier that day at River Days.

Brandy hit Ashley out of nowhere, I hit Dora and Candice handled Asia. When security first broke up the fight they told us we had to leave. They let Asia, Ashley, and Dora leave first. They waited about ten or fifteen minutes before they let us leave. But once we got into Hart Plaza the fight started back up. It didn't stop until the police came over and arrested all six of us. They tried to charge me with attempted murder because Dora was supposed to be pregnant. But I was so happy they let me bail out. I was mad that I still had to go to court because of that shit. That was another reason I wanted to beat Dora's ass. I didn't know nor did I care if they were out. But when I saw her again I already promised myself I was gone kill her ass.

"Man, that dude that was with Gee is so cute, I need to get his number." Candice said snapping me out of my thoughts.

"That's Chris. He got a baby with Ashley and the girl we saw him with today." I said.

"Damn, he can give me a baby too." Candice said.

"You are so funny." I said laughing.

"Girl, I'm serious. My daughter dead beat ass daddy ain't doing shit for her." Candice said.

"Speaking of baby daddies. Candice, have you talked to your brother?" Brandy asked.

"Hell no, not since he gave me money for Cathy." Candice said.

"I called him like five times. He usually always answers his phone when I call. And if he don't, he calls me right back." Brandy said.

"You know how he is." Candice said.

"Yeah, I know I'm just worried about him." Brandy said.

"You are still in love with him aren't you?" I asked her.

"Girl yes, he's my first love and the father of my son. And after all the times he's cheated on me I'm still around." She said, and I could tell she wanted to cry.

"I say we all got back to my place. I need to sleep in my damn bed. Y'all can either share the guest room or one of y'all can take the sofa." I said.

"Sounds like a plan to me. I'll sleep on the sofa." Candice stated.

When we got to my house, Mike was sitting in front of the door in the chair that I kept out there.

"What are you doing here Mike?" I asked him.

"I came to see you." He said as he stood up.

"Really Mike? The last time you came to see me you didn't want anything but a place to lay yo head for the day." I said as I opened the door. Brandy and Candice walked in and closed the door behind them.

"Can we go inside and talk?" He asked.

"I have company as you can see." I said.

"I don't care. My boys use to be over my crib when you came over. We can go in your room." He said.

"Fine, but we're not fucking." I said.

"Jasmine, I didn't say shit about fucking." He said smiling as I opened the door. We walked inside, and he closed and locked the door.

"Girl, it feels so good in here." Brandy said.

"Bran, you know where everything is." I said as I walked into my room with Mike following me. "We can talk after I get out the shower." I said as I walked into the bathroom to turn the water on.

"Whatever floats ya boat." He said as I smiled.

Daivon

I was just getting out the shower waiting for Gee to come over. I texted him and asked him was he still coming, but he hasn't text back yet. Tim left before I got in the shower. He said he had something to handle. I told him that I would be out and about just in case he finished doing what he had to do while Gee was over here. I was sitting on the bed watching TV when someone banged on the door.

"Who is it?" I asked as I got off the sofa. No one answered. "Who the fuck is it?" I asked again as I got in front of the door. I looked through the peephole and saw Gee was standing there with a scowl on his face.

"What the fuck took you so long to open the door?" He asked as he walked past me and into the house.

"Well, if you would have said your fucking name we wouldn't have had any problems." I said as I walked past him and walked in my room.

"What the fuck ever. What the fuck did you want me to come over here for? I told yo ass I wasn't fucking you again." He said.

"Who said anything about fucking? I told you what I wanted." I said smiling.

“And what’s that? For me to tell Je’leese?” He asked me.

“Or I’ll tell her, it’s your choice. Just know if I tell Je’leese, Katherine is going to know about Chris’ part in it also.” I said.

“Nah, I don’t think I’ll choose any of them.” He said.

“Then what the fuck are you going to do? Je’leese is going to find out that I’ve fucked her fiancé three times. And like I said, it’s either you tell her or I’ll tell her.” I said.

“No Je’leese isn’t going to find out you fucked her husband bitch.” He said.

“Y’all didn’t get married yet, so whatever.” I said.

“Think again bitch, we got married yesterday along with Chris and Katt. Now I’m leaving.” He said as he walked out my room.

“You leave and I send the copy of those photos too her.” I said, he turned back around and looked at me like he wanted to kill me.

“What do I have to do in order for you not to tell Je’leese?” He asked.

I didn’t answer him; I just walked over to him and dropped to my knees. I unbuttoned his pants and pulled his dick out and started to suck it.

"Do this feel good?" I asked him as I started to lick his balls. He didn't answer me, but I knew it felt good because he started to breathe hard.

"Shut the fuck up." He said as he rammed his dick down my throat.

Katherine

I was sitting on the bed waiting on Chris to get out the shower so we could go get some breakfast. I was about to turn on the TV when my phone rang. I got off the bed and walked over to the table where it was charging. It was Je'leese.

"Hello." I answered.

"I see you forgot you was supposed to be going to the doctor's office with me." She said.

"Aww, I'm sorry boo. I had a long night with Christopher." I said.

"It's cool. I had a long night with Giovanni but somehow he still got me up. I'm almost here now." She said.

"Call me when you leave there. Christopher and I should be done with breakfast by then." I said.

"Okay, I'm going over to the apartment. Daivon texted me asking me was I still coming over." She said.

"Well, call me when you get over there." I said.

"Okay." She said and we hung up the phone. Just as I was putting the phone back on the charger Chris was walking out the bathroom.

"I was thinking, maybe we should take Chris and Christina out to breakfast with us. Then we can all go shopping." Chris said.

"That's cool. I don't have a problem with that." I said.

"Can you call mama and tell her to have them ready?" He asked.

"Sure." I said as I picked up my phone back up and looked through my contacts for Christopher's mother name. Once I found her name I pressed dial. The phone rang three times before she answered.

"Hello." She said.

"Hey mama, Christopher said can you get Lil Chris and Christina ready. We're about to take them to breakfast, and shopping." I said.

"I'm glad he finally told you. I wanted to tell you yesterday baby. Please forgive me for keeping that from you." She said.

"It's okay, I know you were keeping the secret because he's your son." I said.

"I'll talk to you some more when you get here. I gotta wake the kids up." She said.

"Okay." I said as we hung up the phone.

“What was she talking about?” Christopher asked me as he put his pants on.

“None of your business.” I said smiling.

“She’s going to tell me anyway.” He said as he stuck out his tongue.

“I bet she won’t.” I said as I walked closer to him.

“My mama loves me, she’s going to tell me.” He said.

“You’re a mama’s boy. But she won’t tell you what we were talking about.” I said as I kissed him

“We’re going to see.” He said.

When we got to Charles and Renee’s house, we both went inside. I talked to Renee while she fixed Christina’s hair and Charles, Lil Chris and Chris were somewhere talking.

“Are you ready to go?” Chris asked me as he appeared in the door way.

“Yeah.” I said, we said our goodbyes to Charles and Renee then walked out the door.

“Mommy, me and Stina had fun last night. Granny and papa took us to Chuckie Cheese and the movies. We saw the Smurfs 2.” Lil Chris said as we walked towards the car.

"That's wonderful baby." I said.

"Stina, come here." Christopher said.

"Yes daddy?" She asked as she walked toward him.

"This is my wife Katherine. She stays in the house that you will be staying in from now on." He said as he picked her up.

"Hi." Christina said as she hid her face behind her hands.

"It's okay Stina. This is my mommy. She's nice and will give us anything we want." Lil Chris said.

"Hi Christina." I said as she moved her hands.

"You're pretty like Lil Chris said you were." Christina said.

I smiled. "Thank you sweetie. You're pretty too." I said. She reached her hands out for me to hold her. I picked her up and we walked to the car.

"Are y'all ready to go out to eat?" Christopher asked us.

"Yes!" Lil Chris and Christina said together. I put Christina in the car and buckled her seat belt as Christopher put Lil Chris in the car and buckled his seat belt.

Je'leese

I was leaving the doctor with some shocking news. I was trying to get in touch with Giovanni, but he wasn't answering his phone. I got on the freeway heading to the apartment to see what Daivon wanted. When I got to the apartment I felt weird, I sat in the car for a few minutes trying to get in touch with Katt or Giovanni, but neither of them was answering the phone. I gave up trying to get in touch with them. I did text Katt and told her to call me when she got a chance, then I got out the car and walked towards the door. When I got there the door was already unlocked so I just walked in. As soon as I stepped inside I heard Giovanni and Dai's voice yelling. They were coming from Dai's room so that's where I walked. I was wondering what the hell was Giovanni doing over here and why were they arguing. Once I got closer I heard everything.

"Daivon, you took advantage of me while I was fucking drunk the second time. And the third time yo hoe ass was black-mailing me." Giovanni said.

"How the fuck did I take advantage of a grown ass man? Yeah we fucked while you were drunk and I was sober. That don't mean I took advantage of yo ass. You wanted it just as much as I did." Daivon said.

"Bitch, you know damn well I didn't want it and if I wasn't drunk I wouldn't have fucked yo nasty ass.

You wanna know the real reason you fucked me and Chris and tried to black-mail me?" Giovanni asked her.

"What's the real reason Gee? Since you know so fucking much what's the real reason?" Dai asked.

"You're jealous of Katt and Leesy so you fucked me and Chris so you could feel like you had something over them. But bitch you don't got shit over them. Chris didn't mean to fuck you and I sure as hell didn't mean to fuck your nasty trifling ass." Giovanni said.

"Maybe I am jealous of them. But that's still beside the point. Both Je'leese and Katherine will find out I fucked their niggas." Dai said.

"Bitch, Je'leese ain't gone know shit, and neither is Katt." Giovanni said. At this point I had tears streaming down my face. I turned around and walked back out the door and back to my car. When I got to my car I grabbed my purse and walked back into the apartment. Giovanni and Dai were still arguing. I took my baby 9mm out the purse and sat the purse on the sofa. I was glad I had a silencer on it. I didn't need anyone to know what I was about to do.

"I swear if Je'leese finds out about this I will kill you." Giovanni said.

"Well it's too bad, I just found out." I said as I walked into the room with my 9 pointed at Daivon.

"Je'leese baby, put the gun down." Giovanni said. But his words fell on deaf ears. "POW!" I pulled the trigger. The bullet hit Daivon right in her forehead. I pointed the gun at Giovanni.

"I loved you." I said as even more tears fell from my face.

"I love you too, please don't do this." Giovanni said.

"Fuck you! But before you die you should know I'm pregnant." I said as I pulled the trigger again. "POW!"

Chris

Me and my lil family were in the car on our way to Tim Horton's so we could eat, then head to Somerset to shop. I was so glad Katt wasn't really mad about Christina.

"I wonder what Dai and Leese can be talking about that she can't answer her phone." Katt said.

"What you mean?" I asked her.

"Leese left me a message telling me to call her, now she's not answering. She's at the apartment with Dai though." Katt said. It took me a few minutes to remember the conversation I had with Gee the yesterday.

"Shit!" I said as I pressed the gas and started to speed on the highway.

"What? Why are you driving so fast?" Katt asked me.

"We need to hurry up and get to the apartment," was all I said.

It took me five minutes to get to the apartment. I saw Je'leese's car parked next to Gee's car.

"What is Gee car doing here?" Katt asked.

"Katherine, stay in the car." I said as I opened the door.

"For what Christopher?" She asked me.

"Just please stay here." I said.

"No I'm not, I'm coming in there with you." She said as she took off her seat belt and opened the door. I sighed.

"Lil Chris and Stina, y'all stay here. Do not get out this car. I'm going to lock the door. Stay right here and don't open the door for anyone besides me or your mama." I said as Lil Chris nodded his head.

"Daddy, where are you going?" Stina asked me.

"I need to handle something real fast. I'll be right back." I said as I locked the door before I closed it. Katt closed her door and followed behind me.

"What is the door opened for?" Katt asked, but I knew something bad had happened. We walked into the house me leading the way. I walked to Daivon's room.

"Shit!" I yelled as I saw Giovanni's body lying on the floor.

"Oh my god!" Katherine screamed.

"He cheated on me with her." A voice said. I looked up and Je'leese sitting on the bed.

"Je'leese, what happened?" I asked her as Katherine stood in the door crying.

"I-I shot both of them. He cheated, I loved him." Je'leese said. Katherine wiped her tears and walked over to the bed. She took the gun from Je'leese's hand and sat it down on the night stand.

"Chris, we need to go! Somebody could have heard the gun shots." Katt said.

I checked Gee's pulse. He was still breathing.

"He's still alive. I need to check Daivon." I said. When I stood fully up Je'leese looked at me.

"If she's not dead let the bitch die. She deserves it." Je'leese said as she finally looked at Daivon's body.

"Okay, look Katt I need you to take the kids to get something to eat, and then go to the house. I'll call you later. I need to take Leese and Gee to the hospital." I said.

"Hospital? For what? There's nothing wrong with me." Je'leese said.

"Leese, you're going. We're driving Gee's car too." I said.

Jasmine

I woke up around one in the afternoon in Mike arms. I couldn't lie, it felt good waking up in a man arms. I couldn't remember the last time I'd done that.

"Good morning." Mike said. I hadn't even realized he was up.

"Good morning." I said smiling.

"Police came here looking for you." He said. My heart nearly stopped.

"What did they want?" I asked him.

"I don't know. Your girls opened the door. They was trying to wake you up after they left. But I told them to let you sleep. You was looking so peaceful." He said. I jumped out the bed. I walked out my room and into the living room.

"What did the police want?" I asked Brandy and Candice who were sitting on the sofa smoking a blunt.

"They wanted to ask you some questions about Gee." Brandy said.

"What about him?" I asked.

"They said he was shot this morning." Candice said.

"Oh my god." I said. I walked over to the sofa and sat down in between them.

"Jas, that dude you got in that room seems like a good dude. Stop worrying about Gee. He's happily engaged." Brandy said. I rolled my eyes.

"Bran, I'm done messing with Gee. But I do want to know if he's okay." I said.

"The police said he was at Sinai, but what about dude in the room?" Candice asked, but I didn't answer her. I just got up off the sofa and walked back into the room.

"What's up?" Mike asked me as he stood up straight. I noticed he was putting on his clothes.

"Are you leaving?" I asked him.

"Yeah, you want to go check on yo boo gone ahead." He said.

"Mike, it's not like that. I just want to make sure he's straight. He made sure I was straight when I got jumped." I said.

"It's cool. Call me later." He said.

"Can you take me? I don't feel like driving." I asked him as I walked up to him.

"Why yo girls can't take you?" He asked me.

"Because, I want to spend some time with you after I check on him. We can go to the movies or something." I said.

"Jasmine, do you have any feelings for the dude at the hospital?" He asked me looking directly into my eyes.

"No I don't. We messed around a few times. He's in a relationship, and I don't want to mess that up for him. I just want to make sure he's okay." I said.

"Aight." He said.

After I showered Mike and I headed to the hospital. When we got there, the woman told me Gee was on the sixth floor; we hopped on the elevator and got off on the sixth floor. As soon as we got off we ran into Chris.

"Chris, what happened? Is he okay?" I asked.

"I don't know what happened, but he's in surgery right now. But look Jasmine, now is not the time for you to be here. Je'leese is here and right now and I don't think I can stop her from killing you. But when Gee get out of surgery I'll tell him you stopped by to see him." Chris said.

"Okay." I said. As soon as I turned around my cell phone was ringing. I pulled it out my pocket. It was Brandy.

“Hello.” I said.

“Jasmine, they killed him. Somebody killed James!” Brandy yelled into the phone.

“Bran, what? What happened?” I asked.

“I’m on my way to Southwest. James’ mama called Candice phone and told her they found his body on Beatrice.” Brandy screamed into the phone.

“Bran, look I’ll come over there. Just call me when you get there.” I said as I looked at Mike.

“What happened?” He asked me as we walked back towards the elevator.

“Brandy’s baby daddy was found dead out there by his house. I’m sorry for canceling on you. But she’s my fam. I need to go be there for her.” I said.

“It’s cool. I’ll come with you.” He said.

I smiled as we got on the elevator.

Katherine

I was at McDonalds with the kids. I really wanted to go check on Je'leese and see if she was okay, and ask her why she thought Daivon slept with Gee.

"Mommy, did you hear me?" Lil Chris asked me snapping me out my thoughts.

"No baby, what did you say?" I asked him.

"We're finished." He said.

"Okay, come on." I said as I grabbed the tray. We walked to the trash and dumped the tray then sat the tray on top of the trash. "Come on, I'm going to take y'all back to granny and papa's house." I said as we walked out the door.

"But I thought we were going shopping." Lil Chris said with a confused look on his face.

"We are. I just need to go check on your nanny." I said.

"Is she okay?" Lil Chris asked.

"She's just sick. She's going to be okay though." I said, but I didn't know if that was the truth or not.

"Okay." Lil Chris said as we made it to the car.

"I want my daddy." Christina said as tears filled her eyes.

"Your daddy is going to come with me to get you from Granny and papa's house. Is that okay?" I asked her as I made sure their seat belts were on.

"Okay." She said with smile.

When we got to Renee and Charles house I told them in so many words what happened. Renee wanted to come to the hospital with me to make sure Gee was okay, but I convinced her to stay there with the kids, and I would call her when I got there. I got back in the car and drove to Sinai Hospital. I wondered if Daivon was really messing with Gee. But it was no telling. Then I wondered if she was dead. My mind was on a million, I couldn't believe it, and everything was good just yesterday. Daivon was dating Tim and Gee was talking about moving out of the state with Leesy, how and when could he have time to cheat with Daivon?

When I got to the hospital, I texted Chris.

"What floor are y'all on?" I asked him. I turned the music up some waiting on him to text back.

"I thought I asked you to go to the house. Why didn't you listen?" He texted back.

"Christopher, my best friend needs me right now. What floor?" I asked him. I really didn't feel like hearing his damn mouth. All he had to do was tell me what floor.

"We're on the sixth floor, I hope you didn't bring the kids." He texted back. I looked at the phone, then put it in my purse and cut the car off. I couldn't believe he would think I'd bring the kids here. When the elevator doors opened for me to get in, Christopher was standing in there.

"Where are the kids?" He asked me as I got on the elevator.

"They're at your parents. I told them what I know, now I want to know what you know." I said to him.

"What do you mean what I know?" He asked as he looked down at the floor.

"Christopher really? Whenever your ass is nervous about something, you always looking down at the floor. Now what the hell do you now?" I asked him as the elevator came to a stop. We both got off and he pulled me to the side away from the nurses and people who were passing by.

"Gee and I fucked Daivon one night while we were drunk. A few weeks later, Gee got drunk again, Daivon was sober and she seduced him. After that, she blacked-mailed him so he would sleep with her. Today she was threatening him telling him she would tell you and Leese everything. But Gee wanted to tell her on his own. Leese overheard everything and she shot Daivon and Gee. She's also three months pregnant." Christopher said in one breath. I just couldn't believe the words that just came out of his mouth. I took a deep breath stopping myself from slapping the shit out of him in this hospital.

"Where is Je'leese?" I asked him as tears filled my eyes. I couldn't believe Gee fucked Dai, and I definitely couldn't believe Christopher fucked her either. Now, all the sadness I felt about her possibly being dead, went right out the window.

"She's in the waiting room. Their doing surgery on Gee." Christopher said as he pointed towards the waiting room. I walked towards the way he pointed. When I got to the waiting room Je'leese was sitting in a chair with her head in her hands. I walked over to her and sat next to her.

"Leese?" I said. She slowly picked her head up. Her eyes were red like she'd been smoking, but I knew it was from her crying. "How are you feeling?" I asked her.

"Hurt. Betrayed." She said as she looked up at Chris who was standing next to me. She didn't tell him anything. She just stared.

"I know you probably hate me Je'leese, but I'm sorry about what happened. And I know you probably don't want to hear this but Gee loved you. He wanted to tell you, but he knew how that you loved Daivon like a sister. That's why he always hated her. She'd send him naked pictures, and freaky text messages. He'd just delete them and try and get you to stop hanging with her." Chris said.

Je'leese looked away. "I don't hate you Chris. I hate myself. I put my trust in the wrong people." Je'leese said as more tears fell from her eyes. I didn't even look at Chris; I didn't have shit to say to him right now. If I had a damn gun I would have shot his ass. "Did you move the body?" Je'leese asked never looking up from the ground.

"I'm trying to make sure my mans is good before I do that." Chris said.

"What happens if the police go there?" I asked not looking at him.

"If the police was called they would have been there before we left. I'm not worried about the police. I cleaned up all evidence indicating we were there. I wiped everything down and I cleaned up Gee's blood." Chris said.

"Chris, go throw that bitch in a river somewhere." Je'leese said as she looked Chris in his eyes.

"What about Gee?" Chris asked.

"I'll be here. I'm not going anywhere." Je'leese said.

“Are you sure?” Chris asked.

“Yeah.” Je’leese said.

“Katt, can you come with me, to make sure everything goes smoothly?” Chris asked me. I wanted to tell him hell no, he can go to hell. But I knew I had to go there and help him out for Je’leese’s sake. I didn’t want her to go to jail for killing a snake ass bitch like Daivon.

“Leese, are you going to be okay here by yourself?” I asked Je’leese. She nodded her head yes, but didn’t say anything. I got up and walked away with Chris.

Je'leese

Not even five minutes after Chris and Katt walked off a doctor walked up. "Family of Giovanni Smith?" He called out.

"Right here." I said.

"Who are you to him?" The doctor asked.

"I'm his wife, my name is Je'leese Smith." I said.

"Well Mrs. Smith, I have some good news, your husband's surgery went fine. He's in recovery right now. We're going to move him into his personal room in about twenty minutes." The doctor said.

"Is he awake?" I asked.

"No. But it's only a matter of time before he wakes up. If you want to be by his side when he does I'll walk you back there." He said. I didn't know what to do, I was torn. I didn't want to be by his side, but then again I did. Maybe it was the baby wanting me to be by his side, because my heart and mind sure as hell didn't want me to be nowhere near that nigga.

"Sure." I said. He turned around and started walking and I followed him. When we got in front of Gee's room I just stood there.

"You can go in." The doctor said. It still took me a few minutes to go in. But I finally did. When I walked in I didn't look at him, I looked at the ground.

"Je'leese?" I heard a voice say, at first I thought it was in my head. "Leesy, is that you?" I heard. I looked up at Giovanni. His eyes were open and he had a worried look on his face. I didn't say anything. I just stood there staring at him. "Je'leese, baby I'm sorry. I didn't know how to tell you." He said.

Here he was laid up in a hospital bed with a gunshot wound from me, and he was the one apologizing. I laughed in my head.

"Can you say something?" He asked me.

"What is there to say?" I asked him looking back down at the ground.

"Say you forgive me or something." He said.

"I don't forgive you Giovanni." I said finally looking back at him.

"Why? I didn't mean to fuck her. The first time, me and Chris ran a train on her, the second time I was just plain ole drunk, and the third time she black-mailed me. I'm sorry." He said.

"Giovanni, you didn't mean to fuck her, but you did. And you kept this away from me instead of just being a man and telling me you got drunk and fucked my best friend. You couldn't say that? What was so hard about saying that? Yeah I would have been mad, but I would have forgiven you. Now I don't want to forgive you. I don't even want to be around you right now. I actually wish you would have died." I said. I was angry I couldn't stop myself. So I went on. "I don't want my child around you. You're a lying, no good, son of a bitch!" I screamed. He didn't say anything. He just laid there with tears in his eyes. I quickly looked away from him. I didn't want them fake ass tears to faze me like saying what I just said fazed me.

"Leesy, I know you're just saying that out of anger. And you're right. I should have been man enough to tell you, but I wasn't. I was scared to lose you. I didn't want to see you walk out of my life." He said.

"Well, now you've lost me. You lost me for good. I don't want shit to do with your ass. The only reason I'm here right now is because Katt and Chris went to clean up the mess I made at the apartment but as soon as they get back, I'm leaving." I said as someone knocked on the door.

"Come in." Giovanni said.

"We're here to move you to your room." The nurse said. Giovanni nodded his head never taking his eyes off me. "Are you okay?" The nurse asked Giovanni. Then she gave me an evil eye like she wanted to say something.

"Yes, I'm fine." He said.

When we got into Giovanni's personal room I sat in the chair looking out the window. The nurse was still in there hooking the machines back up. She kept glancing over at me and I was getting sick of her ass.

"Bitch, why the fuck you keep looking at me? Do you have some shit to say?" I asked her.

"Leesy, calm down." Giovanni said, but I gave him a stare and he knew not to say shit else to me. The nurse didn't say anything; she didn't even look at me anymore.

"Scary bitch." I said as she walked to the door. She didn't even turn around as she walked out the door.

"Je'leese, don't take your anger out on other people. I'm the one you're mad at." Giovanni said.

"The bitch shouldn't have kept looking at me. And I wish you'd stop talking to me." I said. I knew I was being a cold hearted bitch, but at this point I really didn't give a fuck about him or his feelings. And he'd made me this way. After all the shit I'd been through with him, I had been through hell and back with his ass, and he betrayed me in the worst way. I wasn't even mad that he got drunk and slept with Daivon twice. The shit I was mad at was that he didn't tell me about it. He had me in the bitch face thinking she was really my friend. But I couldn't be mad at anybody but myself. I was too damn nice. But I bet you I won't be from here on out.

"Je'leese, do you really plan on keeping my child away from me? You know I grew up without my pops. I don't want my seed to go through the same thing I went through." He said.

"Then you should have thought about that while you was drinking." I said not even looking over at him. I knew if I looked at him he was gone have tears in his light brown eyes, and I was going to feel even worse for the things I was saying, but I wanted him to hurt just like I was hurting.

"Je'leese, please." He said. But I didn't reply.

Chris

Katt was driving back to the hospital after we dropped Daivon's body in the Detroit river. I made sure the bullet was out of her head before we tossed it. I didn't want any traces being led back to Je'leese. I wanted to say something to Katt to make sure that she wasn't going to leave me. But she was mad as hell and I didn't know what to say to her.

"Katt, are you okay?" I asked her. She looked at me like she wanted to kill me.

"What you think? A girl who I thought was my best friend fucked my husband. Do you think I would be okay? Honestly Chris the only thing that's stopping me from leaving yo ass right now is Lil Chris. If I didn't have him I wouldn't be sitting here having this conversation with you." She said.

"Katherine, baby I'm sorry. The next morning when I woke up and realized what happened I regretted it. I wished it had never happened. I'm just glad she didn't black-mail me like she did Gee." I said.

"Christopher, I wish you'd shut the fuck up right now." Katt said as she pulled into the parking garage of the hospital. And I did just that. I didn't want her ass to get any ideas and kill me in this damn garage. I took out my phone and called Je'leese's cell phone.

"Hello." She asked.

"Is he out of surgery?" I asked.

"Yeah, his tired ass is out of surgery. We're still on the sixth floor. In room six ten." She said.

"Ight, me and Katt on our way up." I said.

"Mhm," was all she said as we hung up the phone.

When we got up to Gee's room Je'leese was sitting by the window looking out of it and Gee was laying in the bed with his eyes on Je'leese.

"How you feel man?" I asked him as I sat down in the chair by his bed. Katt walked over and stood by Je'leese.

"Man, I'm just grateful that I'm still alive, all I could think about when they were trying to get this bullet out my chest was seeing my child grow up." Gee said.

"Yo ass ain't gone see my fucking child. You don't deserve to, how many times do I have to tell you that?" Je'leese asked. All of our eyes were on her as she stared at Gee with evil eyes.

"Leese, come on. Don't do that." I said.

"He couldn't even be a man and tell me he slept with my best friend. You think I'm gone let him around my child?" She asked not taking her eyes off him.

“Leese, you’re just upset right now.” Katt said.

“No, I’m serious. I don’t even want to be here right now. Katt, can you take me to your house?” She asked Katherine.

“Yeah, I gotta go get the kids first though.” Katherine said.

“That’s fine. I just don’t want to be around his ass.” Je’leese said as she got up and walked out the door.

“Gee, don’t worry about what she was saying. She’s just saying it out of anger. I just did the same thing. But she knows no matter what she loves you and she’ll never leave you. Just like I love Christopher and will never leave him. Get well though. And we’ll be at the house if y’all need me.” Katt said walking out the door. I was glad she said that. I even smiled a lil bit.

“Man, what the hell happened?” I asked Gee once the door was closed.

“I was over the apartment or whatever and Daivon was talking about sending them pictures to Leese and telling Katt how she fucked both of us. I asked her what I had to do so she wouldn’t do that, she got on her knees and sucked me up. After she did that, she stood up and said she wanted to fuck me. I told her fuck no, I wasn’t going to cheat on Je’leese especially now that she was my wife. We got to arguing. The next thing I know Je’leese standing behind us with her baby in her hand. And you should know what happened next." He said.

"Did Leese see her suck you off?" I asked him.

"I don't think she did. I mean if she did, she would have shot us right then and there." He said.

"Man, that shit is crazy as hell. I'm kind of happy the bitch dead." I said.

"Shit, I'm not kind of, I am happy. The bitch deserved to be dead." Gee said.

"When Katt told me Je'leese was on her way over there from the doctor's office, I got there as quick as I could. But not quick enough." I said.

"I heard everything. I hurt her man. I hurt her to the point where she told me she hated me and wished I would have died. Man you don't know what that did to me." He said as tears formed in his eyes.

"Man you know Je'leese loves you. And you also know females say things when they're hurt, and don't forget she's pregnant so her hormones are all over the place." I said.

"I know man, but I just didn't know what to say when she said that I couldn't see my seed grow up." He said.

“She’s just talking that bullshit. But we really do need to jet up outta this place before that body wash up on land.” I said.

“Man, get the tickets and shit. My first day outta here I wanna be gone. Leese has been talking to this realtor in ATL. We can move there.” Gee said.

“Aight let me make some calls and ask the nurse when you’re going to be discharged and we can get the tickets handled.” I said as I got up and walked towards the door. “And oh yeah, I’m glad you’re still here man.” I said as I walked out the door.

Jasmine

It'd been four days since they found James' body and nobody knew who killed him. Candice and Brandy had been sleeping over my house along with Mike. He hadn't left my side yet. I'm kind of happy he hadn't either. But today he went to chill with his twins while I spent some time with Candice and Bran.

"I can't believe somebody took him away from me." Brandy said as we sat on my sofa smoking some loud.

"I can't believe it either. Man when mama called me it felt like a piece of me left." Candice said.

"A piece of me did leave. I can't even look at Brandon anymore. He looks just like James. When Brandon and his brothers found out I just broke down all over again." Brandy said as tears fell down her face.

"But my nephews are going to be good though and we're going to find out who killed my brother, they're going to join him." Candice said as she passed me the blunt. I didn't say anything. I just let them vent.

"Where did Mike ass go?" Brandy asked me.

"I'm surprised his ass isn't blowing up your phone like he normally does when he's away from you." Candice said as she laughed.

“He went to chill with his kids.” I said looking down at my phone.

“Well at least he take care of his kids. My baby daddy don’t do shit for Cathy, and that nigga work at Ford, so you know he getting paid.” Candice said. I was listening to them talk, but I was also paying attention to my phone.

“Hey, are you okay?” I sent Mike. I looked up only for a brief second to pass the blunt to Brandy.

“Yeah I’m smooth. Why you ask that?” He texted back.

“I was just checking on you.” I said.

“Oh naw, I’m good shorty. I’ll be through there in like ah hour. You and yo girls get dressed. I’m taking y’all to ah lil get together at my mans Tim crib.” He texted, I smiled.

“Okay.” I said.

“Who yo ass over there talking to got you smiling like that.” Brandy asked me.

“Girl, Mike he said for us to get dress, he’s taking us to a lil get together.” I said.

“I don’t feel like going out.” Brandy said.

“Come on Bran, let’s just go. I know your mind is on my brother, but just go out. Sitting around moping isn't going to make it any better. And it's not going to bring him back." Candice said.

"She's right." I said.

"Fine." Brandy said. I smiled.

An hour later we were pulling up to a house out in Redford.

"I've been too this house before. With James." Brandy said as her eyes started to well up with tears.

"Bran, remember the conversation we had earlier." I said.

"Okay." She said as she wiped the tears away before they could fall. We all got out the car and Mike met me in front. He grabbed my hand and we walked inside. When we got inside there were only a few people in there. They were all standing around the huge living room smoking and drinking.

"Yo, I gotta go holla at my mans real quick. I'll be back." Mike said to me. He kissed my cheek then walked away.

"Girl, where has that nigga been all your life?" Candice asked me as we moved our hips to the music that was playing.

"Shit, he's been playing around. I was fucking with him before I was messing with Gee. He wasn't ready for a relationship." I said.

"But you started messing with Gee who was already in a relationship." Brandy said.

"Yeah, but I wasn't messing with Gee because I loved him. I was messing with him because his dick was good and his money was long." I said laughing.

"Whose dick is better, Mike or Gee's?" Candice asked me.

"No lie, Mike's is better. But Gee's money is longer." I said as we all laughed.

"So, you love Mike?" Brandy asked me.

"Yeah." I said as I looked around the room until I saw Mike standing across the room talking too two dudes. He looked up at me and smiled, I smiled back.

"Girl, I'd say that nigga ready to commit now." Brandy said. I looked at her, then back at Mike. He was walking towards us with the two niggas he was just talking to.

"Jas, Brandy, Candice these are my niggas Tim and Moe." He said as he pointed each of the dudes out.

"Hey." Me, Brandy, and Candice said at the same time.

"I'm sorry about yo lost. James was my nigga." The dude name Tim said to Brandy.

"How did you know James?" Candice asked. Tim looked at Mike.

"That's his sister." Mike said.

"Me and him did business together. He worked with me." Tim said.

"And what did y'all do?" Brandy asked.

"Come on ma, don't play like you don't know what yo man did for a living." Tim said.

"I know what he did for living. And what he did, got him killed." Brandy said.

"I know, and I'm working on finding out who did that to him because they are going to join him." Tim said.

"When you find out who did it, let me know. I want a piece of him." Candice said.

"I got you ma." Tim said as he smiled at Candice.

Katherine

"Je'leese, can you please eat something, you've hardly eaten anything and that's not good for the baby." I said to Je'leese as we sat in the house we now owned in Atlanta.

"Katt, I'm not hungry." Je'leese said as we sat in the dining room at the table. We'd been in Atlanta since Gee was discharged from the hospital a week ago. As soon as we got down there I made a doctor's appointment for Je'leese to make sure the baby was okay. And the baby was fine. Everyone was happy about that. But no one was happy about the tension in the house. The only ones who didn't notice the tension were Lil Chris and Christina. I was glad they were too young to understand the situation at hand. Gee still needed help with some things, and since Leese wouldn't help him, me and Chris had to.

"Leese, you're starving the baby. You have to eat at least two full meals a day, you heard what the doctor said. And I cook every day so you can't complain about not having any food." I said.

"I eat some of it. But I just lose my appetite as soon as I see Giovanni's ass." She said as she rubbed her growing belly.

"Je'leese, when are you going to forgive him?" I asked her.

"Never. I forgave his ass too many times, and this time he don't deserve my forgiveness." She said.

I sighed. I was happy when I heard the front door open and close.

"Mommy, where are you at?" I heard Lil Chris ask.

"I'm in the dining room sweetie." I said. Lil Chris, Christina, Christopher and Gee all walked into the dining room.

"Guess what mommy?" Lil Chris said.

"What?" I asked him as he walked over to me.

"Me and Stina are going to school." He said as he smiled.

"Really?" I asked him.

"Yes!" Lil Chris said.

"The name of the school is Garden Hills. It's only a six minute drive from the house." Christopher said.

"Well, I'm glad the school situation is taken care of. Now we just need to shop for clothes and more furniture." I said.

"I'm hungry." Christina said.

"Stina, you and Lil Chris go wash up. Dinner is almost ready." I said looking at the clock on the wall. I had about two more minutes until my Roast Beef was done. Je'leese got up from the table.

"Where are you going?" I asked her.

"I lost my appetite." She said.

"Je'leese, you need to stop this bullshit. Gee is already hurt because he hurt you. Can't you see this man loves you?" Chris said to her.

Je'leese turned around and looked at Chris. "That's good, the bastard should be hurting. As much pain as he caused me, he's lucky he's still breathing right now."

"That's enough Je'leese. You need to stop this. I get that you're angry, but you can't keep doing this. You're starving yourself and the baby because Gee hurt you. While you're being spiteful you need to think about that baby you have in your stomach." I said.

"If it's that much of a problem from me being here then I'll just get a room at a hotel." Gee said.

"Well, would you hurry up and do that?" Je'leese asked as she walked away.

Giovanni

I couldn't believe how far things had gone between Je'leese and me. I think I really lost the girl I fell in love with, and she was being replaced by a cold hearted woman. But I couldn't be mad at anybody but myself because I created the cold hearted woman she was becoming. For the last three days I'd been staying in Grand Hyatt hotel. It wasn't where I wanted to be. But if I got Je'leese to think about our child instead of the pain that I caused her, then I would be living there until my child was born. I wished she'd stop playing games when it came to my child though. She wouldn't tell me anything about the appointments. She wouldn't tell me when she was due; she wouldn't even tell me the sex of the baby. She wouldn't tell me shit, and that was pissing me off. I knew I did some fucked up things to her, but she was taking it too far. She knew how I feel about being there for my kid, and she was using that to hurt me. I just knew she was. I was glad I still had Katherine. She was keeping me up on the news about my baby. Even though she wouldn't tell me the sex or the due date she told me damn near everything else. I was snapped out of my thoughts by my phone ringing. It was Chris.

"Hello." I said.

"What's the word?" He asked me.

"Shit, sitting in this damn room bored." I said shaking my head.

"We heading to Lenox, you down?" He asked.

"Who is we?" I asked him.

"Everyone, we're taking the kids shopping." Chris said.

"Man, I really don't feel like hearing Je'leese talk about how much she hates me." I said.

"She's going to be cool. She know this trip is for y'all god children. She promised to be on her best behavior. So come to the house." He said.

"Aight man, I'll be there." I said.

"Fasho." He said as we hung up the phone.

When I got to the house Chris came outside with Lil Chris tagging along with him, they got in my car. Je'leese, Katt and Christina came out the house next. I looked at Je'leese who had a bag of Cheese Puffs in her hand. She was bigger than the last time I'd seen her. She was really beautiful pregnant. I couldn't help but smile.

"Hey Parian." Lil Chris said.

"Wassup man? How you been?" I asked him as I turned around to look at him.

"Good, where you been? My nanny been missing you." He said.

"I've been at work. And how you know she's been missing me?" I asked him smiling.

"Because she told me and Stina yesterday. And she also said y'all were having a baby." He said.

"Yeah, we're having a baby. You're going to have a lil god brother or sister soon." I said.

"I can't wait. If it's a girl I'm going to protect her and Stina, and if it's a boy me and him gone protect Stina." He said.

"That's right son." Chris said as we both laughed.

"How she been?" I asked Chris.

"She been good. But on the real, she do miss you, and she worries about you." Chris said as Katt pulled out the driveway and I followed her.

"Worry about me for what? And how do you know she misses me?" I asked him. I ain't no sucka but I was glad she was missing me.

"She worries that you're still in pain from the shot, and since you left she asks me have I talked to you every hour. I had to tell her that I wasn't supposed to talk to you every hour. Man she snapped on me so quick. I just laughed." He said as I chuckled.

"Man, I really do miss her. I just wish things could go back to normal, or she go back to normal." I said.

"Give her a few more weeks. She's getting there." He said.

"Parian, what's your favorite football team?" Lil Chris asked me.

"Man, I'm a Saints fan. If it ain't about the Saints then I don't want to hear it." I said as I laughed.

"My daddy like the Falcons, he said that he's going to get us some tickets to go to a game." Lil Chris said.

"Yo daddy know how I feel about them 'Dirty Birds' and I'll only go to a Falcons game if they're playing the Saints." I said.

"What's a dirty bird?" Lil Chris asked.

"It's the nickname people gave to the Falcons." Chris said as we both laughed.

"Do the Saints even play the Falcons this season?" I asked him.

"They play the Saints their first game of the regular season." Chris said. We talked about football the rest of the way to the mall.

Jasmine

Mike and I were getting back to being close like we once were as the weeks went by. We were trying to see if a relationship between us could last this time. While I was spending my time with Mike, Candice was spending her time with Tim and Brandy was spending her time with Moe. Even though she told us she wasn't ready to be in a relationship so soon after losing the love of her life, she still went on dates with Moe. We even went out on dates together.

Me, Candice, and Brandy were in Kiss getting our toes and nails done when the news came on.

"Aye, that's Je'leese best friend." I said looking at the picture of Daivon on the screen.

"Well, the picture said she was found in the river." Brandy said.

"Man, this a fucked up city." Candice said.

"Hell yeah, I can't wait until I move out of Detroit. But I wonder what happened to her." I said.

"We'll never know, and where yo ass thinking about going?" Brandy asked me.

"I haven't decided yet." I said.

"Y'all look ain't that Dora and her cousins?" Candice said.

"Hell yeah it is." I said as they walked into the shop.

"I'm not even coming here no more if bitches like that come here." Brandy said loud enough where they could hear her.

"Bitch, who the fuck you talking about?" Ashley asked.

"Ash, let it go. We're better than them hoes." Dora said.

"Y'all better than us but yo pregnant ass was fighting!" I said.

"Jasmine ain't nobody come in here to argue with yo rat ass." Asia said.

"Bitch, do it look like I give a fuck what y'all came in here to do? I ain't finish with you hoes by a long shot." I said.

"Bitch it's funny that you got so much mouth when yo friends around but when it's just you, yo ass is quiet as a fucking mouse." Ashley said.

"Bitch, it doesn't matter. From now on she's going to have us with her. So what y'all want to do?" Brandy asked.

"Bitch, didn't we just say we don't want to fight y'all hoes. But when I drop this baby best believe I'm whopping yo ass Jasmine." Dora said.

"Bitch, go find yo baby daddy." I said laughing.

"Don't worry about it. Mike gone take care of this one just like he take care of his twins." She said as her and her girls laughed.

"What the fuck are you talking about?" I asked her.

"Come on y'all. I don't want to even get my nails done here." Dora said ignoring me. She and her cousins walked out the nail shop still laughing. I was mad as hell; I wanted to know if Mike was fucking this bitch!

"Jasmine, don't listen to that bitch. She's probably just saying that to get under your skin." Candice said. But I let what she said go through one ear and out the other because it did get under my skin.

As soon as we were done getting our nails done we went back to my house. I went straight in my room and called Mike's phone. He didn't answer so I called him again, he didn't answer that time either. As I was dialing a third time a text message came through. It was from Mike.

"I'm handling some business, what's up ma?" He asked me.

"You got that bitch Dora pregnant?" I texted back.

"Where is this coming from ma? I fucked the bitch but I ain't her baby daddy!" He texted back, I gave a sigh of relief. I was still mad he fucked the bitch, but I was just glad he said he wasn't the baby daddy. But then again I should have known the bitch wouldn't have known who her baby daddy was. She tried to get me to help her trap Gee.

"What are you thinking about?" Candice asked me as she and Brandy walked into my room.

"Dora and this whole pregnant situation. Mike just said he fucked her, but he's not her baby daddy." I said.

"You shouldn't have asked him that in the first place. You know how that bitch is. Didn't she say Gee was her baby daddy too?" Brandy asked.

"Yeah, I thought about that after I texted him." I said.

"I can't wait until I see Ashley ass again. I ain't letting that bitch walk away." Brandy said.

"I'm waiting on Dora ass to drop that fucking baby." I said.

“That bitch might not be pregnant. Cathy’s daddy thought he was having another baby while me and him was still together, but the girl was faking pregnant. She had the fake belly and everything. Girl when I found out I beat the brakes off that bitch.” Candice said.

“I really do miss James. I don’t know what I’m going to do without him.” Brandy said.

“Bran, you gotta be strong, don’t forget you got Lil Brandon. He needs you to be strong.” I said.

“And don’t worry we’re going to send him some company as soon as we find out who killed my brother.” Candice said.

Je'leese

It was the beginning of August and the day before I was supposed find out what I was having. I want a little boy. But Katt and Chris want a god daughter. I didn't ask nor did I care what Giovanni wanted. As far as I was concerned, our relationship was over. We had nothing to talk about. If I wanted him to know anything about my child I'd tell Katt and Chris to let him know. Even though they didn't agree with the way I was doing things, they still told him so he could be up to date. I wasn't mad at him anymore, but I couldn't forgive him, hell his ass didn't deserve my forgiveness. I really tried not to think about him. I was trying to put all my attention my child that would be arriving in a few months. But all my thoughts went back to the day I shot and killed Daivon and tried to kill Giovanni. I thought about all the things I'd said to him in the hospital. The only thing that kept my mind off Giovanni was shopping for my child, and getting the nursery together. I couldn't get the things that I really wanted to get because I didn't know what I was having, but as soon as I left the doctor's office tomorrow I was going shopping and buying real clothes for him or her.

I was sitting in the family room watching Days of Our Lives. Lil Chris and Christina were in school, Katt was working at the mall and Chris was somewhere with

Giovanni. Or at least I thought he was until Giovanni walked through the front door.

"Oh, I didn't know you were here. I came to get a few things." He said. I didn't say anything to him. I turned my attention back to the television. But I could still see him standing there looking at me. When it went on commercial I looked at Giovanni. "I'm sorry. I didn't mean to stare. It's just that your stomach has gotten bigger since the last time I saw you." He said. It had been a few weeks since I'd really seen Giovanni. Whenever he would come to the house I'd always be shopping or in my room. I couldn't lie he looked good as hell right now. He had on a white wife beater, his hair was freshly cut, and he had on some cargo shorts, with some Adidas slippers. I started to get wet just from looking at him. "When is your next doctor's appointment?" He asked, snapping me out of my thoughts.

"Tomorrow." I said as I stood up, I walked towards the kitchen and I heard him following.

"That's when you find out what you're having right?" He asked.

"Yeah." I said as I walked to the ice box. I grabbed the fruit salad that I made me that morning and sat it on the counter.

"I got a few small things for the baby. They're in my car." He said.

"That's nice." I said as got a fork from the dish washer.

"Je'leese, why won't you look me in my eyes?" He asked me. I finally looked into his eyes.

"Giovanni, what do you want?" I asked him.

"I want to have a proper conversation with you. I'm tired of you cursing me out, or you telling me how much you hate me and all the other things you've said. I know I hurt you, and I'm sorry. I really am. I just don't know what to do anymore. You're telling me I can't see my child. Je'leese that hurts more than anything, it hurt more than you telling me you wished I would have died, and you know that hit me hard." He said as tears welled up in my eyes. Damn these hormones! "Leesy, I'll do anything, just please don't keep my child away from me." He said, it was something about the way he called me Leesy, I hadn't heard that in a while.

"Giovanni, I don't plan on keeping you from your child! And I'm sorry for all the harsh things I've said to you. It was only out of anger." I said as I sighed.

"I understand why you said it, and I really am sorry for what I did and how I handled it. You were right when you said I wasn't man enough to tell you what happened. I wasn't at the time. But I am man enough to stand here and tell you I was wrong, and I can understand if you want to get a divorce." He said as the tears finally fell from my eyes, he walked over to me and wiped them away. This was the first time he'd touched me since our wedding night.

"Giovanni?" I said as I looked into his eyes.

"Huh?" He said.

"Make love to me." I said.

"My pleasure." He said as he grabbed my face and kissed me with passion, passion that had never left. It'd been almost two months since he'd touched me and the passion was still there. He broke the kiss, took me by my hand, and led me out the kitchen, through the family room, and up the stairs. We went into my room.

"Wow." He said as he looked around at the baby things I had stacked against the walls. He then turned his attention back to me as I got on the bed. He climbed on the bed too. I was taking off the shirt and shorts I had on, I didn't have on a bra so he started to suck on my breast.

"Mmm." I moaned. As he was sucking on my breast he was pulling down the boy shorts I was wearing. He started trailing kisses down my stomach to my pussy. He opened my legs and kissed and licked the inside of my thighs. He then went face first into my pussy. I arched my back and grabbed the sheets as he pleased me with his tongue. He was nibbling on my clit which was driving me insane.

"Ooooh Babbbyyyyy, I'm cuming." I said as my body started to shake. I was entering the place where I missed being. I exploded all over Giovanni's face he got up and came to kiss me as our tongues danced around. I really wanted to feel him now, and I wasn't going to waste any time. I grabbed his dick and placed it between my legs. He moved my hand out the way as he guided himself into me.

"Ooooh." I gasped.

"Damn girl. I've missed this pussy!" He said as he stroked in and out of me.

"This feels so good." I moaned.

"You missed me?" He asked me as he started stroking faster and harder.

"God Yessss Giovannniiii!" I yelled. I was grinding my hips along with his rhythm.

"Who does this pussy belong too?" He asked me as I felt myself about to cum again.

"Youuu, it belongs toooo yoooouuuu." I yelled as I came all over his dick.

"I'm cuming." He said as he gripped my waist and threw his head back. We were both breathing hard. He pulled out of me and leaned down and kissed me on my lips. I kissed him back, but I was tired and ready for my daily nap.

"Don't leave." I said as he moved from between my legs.

"I won't." He said as he lay on the side of me. I turned around so my back was facing him. He put his arm around me and pulled me closer. He started rubbing my stomach as I fell asleep. I'd missed being in his arms.

When I woke up later that night Giovanni wasn't in the bed with me, but his shirt was still on my bed. I got out the bed and went into the bathroom so I could take a shower. I turned the shower on, put my hair in a messy bun on the top of my head, and then got in the shower. After I was done I wrapped the towel around my body, even though it really didn't fit around me due to my belly. I walked out the bathroom and into my room. I put some clothes on which were some jogging pants and a tank top, put on my house shoes, and walked out the room. When I got downstairs Katt, Chris, and Giovanni were sitting in the computer room.

"What are y'all doing in here?" I asked them. Giovanni looked at me and smiled.

"Chris was looking for some empty buildings that he could buy." Katt said.

"So, I see everything is back to normal with you and my mans." Chris said as he looked at me and laughed. I didn't even respond to what he said. As far as I was concerned things couldn't go back to normal with me and Giovanni. I didn't know how to make things normal with us.

"Leesy, I can't go with you to the doctor's I have to work a double." Katt said.

"It's cool." I said as I sat down on the lazy boy that was in there.

"I'll go with you if you want me to." Giovanni said.

"Okay." I said not looking at him, I looked at Katt and saw she was smiling.

"I put your fruit salad back in the ice box." Giovanni said.

"Thanks." I got up and walked into the kitchen. Katt followed behind me.

"So, what happened?" She asked me.

"Hormones." I said as I got my bowl of fruit salad out the ice box, grabbed a fork, and sat down at the table.

"So, there's no chance of y'all rekindling?" She asked me with a hopeful look on her face.

"I don't think so. But I do know I'll let him be there for his child." I said.

"He loves you Je'leese." Katt said looking at me.

"I love him too. But he hurt me to the core." I said as tears formed in my eyes.

"Leese, Chris did the same thing. He even had a child outside of our relationship and hid her from me for damn near three years." She said.

"Katt, he slept with Daivon once. Giovanni slept with her more than once." I said.

"Yeah, and he was drunk one of them times, and the other time she black-mailed him." She pointed out.

"I don't care about all that. He wasn't man enough to tell me. He hid it from me." I said trying my hardest not to let the tears escape from my eyes. "Look Katt, I don't want to talk about that. Every time I think about him fucking her I think about killing her." I said as I wiped away the tears before they could fall.

"I'm sorry. I don't mean to make you upset. I just want you to know and understand that he still loves you and wants to be with you." She said.

"I understand and I know." I said.

Giovanni

I was driving Je'leese to her doctor's appointment, I couldn't lie I was happy as hell. It was the day she found out what she was having. She hadn't said anything to me since she asked me not to leave her room the day before.

"Are you okay?" I asked her as I turned into the hospital's parking garage.

"Yes, I'm fine." She said looking out the window.

"Are we okay?" I asked her, I know I probably sounded like a soft nigga, but Je'leese is the love of my life and I didn't want her to divorce me.

"No we're not okay. But I don't want to talk about that right now." She said as I parked the car. We both got out the car and walked to the elevator. When we got inside she signed herself in as I sat down in one of the chairs, after she finish signing in she came to sit next to me. I had my phone out and was looking through the few contacts I had. I was about to put my phone away when a text message came through.

"Wassup stranger? Long time no hear from." Jasmine said.

"Nothing much. How you been?" I texted back.

"I've been good. Just living life. Did y'all hear about yo girl best friend Daivon?" She asked and my heart started pounding hard as shit. I looked over at Je'leese and she was reading a book she'd brought with her.

"No, what happened?" I asked. But I had a feeling what she was about to say.

"She was found dead in the Detroit River, her father has been on the news asking has anyone seen or talked to yo girl. They think she's missing or some shit like that." She said. I didn't even text her back. I put the phone in my pocket and looked at Je'leese. She had her long hair down and the earrings I brought her for Christmas last year.

"Mrs. Smith?" A nurse called. Je'leese put the book in her purse and stood up. I followed behind her as we walked through the doors.

"How are you doing today?" The nurse asked Je'leese.

"I'm fine. Just ready to find out what I'm having." Je'leese said smiling.

"Where's the god mama? She couldn't come today?" The nurse asked looking at me.

"No she had to work, but this is my husband and the father Giovanni." Je'leese said as she looked at me.

"Nice to finally meet you Mr. Smith, my name is Amber." The nurse said.

"Nice to meet you too." I said as she checked Je'leese's vitals.

"Your pressure is high, you should already know Dr. Gibson will say something about that." Amber said.

"I know. I've been trying to stay away from things that stress me out." Je'leese said looking at me for a second before she looked at the ground.

"Everything else is fine. I'll get Dr. Gibson. She should be right in." Amber said.

"Okay." Je'leese said as Amber walked out the room.

"Do I make your pressure high?" I asked her as soon as the nurse walked out the room.

"I don't know, but thinking about what you did and how bad you hurt me makes it high." She said as she looked out the window that was next to the bed.

"I really am sorry Je'leese." I said.

"Yeah, you've said that before." She said.

"And I will keep saying it until you know just how sorry I am." I said as a doctor walked into the room.

"Hello." She said.

"Hello Doc." Je'leese said.

"I'm guessing this is the lucky man in your life." Dr. Gibson said as she extended her hand to me.

"I'm Giovanni, and I'm the lucky one." I said as I looked at Je'leese.

"Good to meet you." Dr. Gibson said as she sat down in her chair in front of the computer screen.

"Mrs. Smith, your pressure is extremely high." She said to Je'leese.

"I know." Je'leese said.

"You know what I told you about that. Daddy, can you help mommy not to be stressed with whatever she's stressed with." Dr. Gibson said to me.

"Yes ma'am. She's going to be stress free as off today." I told her. She smiled as she looked at the computer.

"You're gaining a lot of weight also." Dr. Gibson said.

"I guess it's because I'm always eating. But before I found out I was pregnant I was hardly eating." Je'leese said. Dr. Gibson was rubbing some gel on Je'leese big stomach. She moved her paddle as she looked at the screen.

"Wow." She said.

"Wow what?" Je'leese asked looking at her. She turned the screen to where we could see it.

"Twins?" Je'leese asked her.

"Yes ma'am. It seems like the second baby was hiding. I guess having her daddy here is what caused her to come out." Dr. Gibson said.

"Her? Do you know the sex of the other baby?" I asked smiling that I had a girl.

"Yes, it's a boy." Dr. Gibson said smiling at Je'leese who, like me, had tears in her eyes. She looked at me and smiled. I smiled back.

"I'll give you two some time alone. Amber will be back in here to set your next appointment. I want you to come every two weeks instead of every month." Dr. Gibson said.

"Okay." Je'leese said.

"And daddy, don't forget about her stressing." She said.

"I won't." I said as she walked out the room.

"I can't believe it. Twins!" Je'leese said, I walked over to her and wiped the tears from her eyes.

“Do you have any names?” I asked her.

“Giovanni Jr. and Jiovanna with a J,” she said smiling.

“I like those names.” I said as she wiped the few tears from my eyes.

After she got her next appointment we went to Golden Coral for a quick meal, then we went to Lenox to shop for the twins.

“I don’t mean to stress you out.” I said.

“It’s cool, and you don’t have to stay at the hotel anymore. I didn’t have a right saying that you shouldn’t be at the house that you helped pay for and where you still help pay bills.” She said as she looked at me.

“Okay. If it’s cool I’ll swing by the hotel to grab my stuff before going home.” I said.

“That’s cool.” She said as she pulled out the book she was reading earlier.

“What’s that you’re reading?” I asked her.

“Between Love and Justice by Danielle Grant. You should read it.” She said, I guess she was trying to be funny.

“Okay, when you’re done with it I’ll read it.” I said as I smiled at her.

When we got in the mall the first store we went to was True Religion where Katt worked so we could tell her the good news.

"What's up y'all?" She asked as she stopped putting clothes on a rack.

"We're having a boy." Je'leese said Katt had a look of disappointment on her face.

"Well guess I'll have to spoil my god son then." She said as she smiled.

"Oh, don't worry you're going to spoil your god daughter to." Je'leese said.

"Oh my gosh, y'all having twins?" Katt asked as she hugged Je'leese.

"Ouch girl. And yes we are." Je'leese said.

"I can't believe it. Are you sticking with the names you told me?" She asked Je'leese.

"No, instead of naming my son Billy John, I'm going to name him Giovanni Jr." Je'leese said as she laughed.

"You planned on naming our son Billy John?" I asked her.

"Billy John or John Billy." She said as she looked at me.

“I’m glad to see y’all talking rather than arguing.” Katt said.

“I am too.” I said.

“It was Giovanni that got little miss Jiovanna to come out of hiding.” Je’leese said.

“I knew you had to be having more than one baby.” Katt said.

“How did you know?” Je’leese asked her.

“Yo ass is too big to be carrying one baby. How long are y’all going to be here?” She asked us.

“Not long, I don’t want to be on my feet all day.” Je’leese said.

“Okay, well can you pick the kids up? Christopher said he wasn’t going to be able to do it. But he said he was going to bring dinner home.” Katt said.

“Yeah, we’ll get them.” I said.

“Thanks y’all and congratulations.” Katt said.

“No problem. And thanks for everything.” I said.

Jasmine

"Are you going to keep ignoring me?" The text from Mike read. I hadn't talked to him since the day I ran into that bitch Dora and her hoe ass cousins.

"No I am not ignoring you. I've just been busy." I lied.

"Jas, why are you lying to me? Yo girls already ratted you out. You haven't been doing shit but sitting around yo house." Mike said.

"Okay fine, I haven't been anything. But I just needed a break. I haven't been feeling good that's all." I said. I was going to slap the shit outta Brandy and Candice for snitching me out like that.

"I'm on my way over there. Tim wants to talk to you and yo girls." Mike said.

"For what? Brandy and Candice are already with him, why can't he just talk to those two?" I asked him.

"I don't know Jasmine damn! Just be ready when I get there." The text said. I sighed, got off the bed, and put some clothes on. I put my hair in a ponytail and got back in the bed. I didn't really feel like doing anything, that's why I'd been staying in the house. I was dozing off when my phone rang.

"Hello." I said.

"Yo, bring yo ass outside." Mike said.

"Alright." I got up grabbed my hoodie and my keys and walked out the house.

"You look good." Mike said as I got in the car.

"Thanks." I said. I had on a simple True Religion jogging fit.

"So, are you going to tell me the real reason you've been ignoring me?" He asked as he pulled off.

"I guess I was mad at the fact you slept with Dora." I said.

"Jas, that was before I fell back in love with you." He said.

"Michael, you were never in love with me, and you're not in love with me now." I said.

"No lie Jasmine, I really was in love with you. And I am right now," he said.

"Then why did you wait so long to come around? And when you did finally come around it was because you needed a place to sleep." I said.

"Look Jasmine, I'm sorry. It took me so long because I was going through some shit with my baby mama. You know she was talking about taking my twins and you know how much I love my kids." He said.

"Yeah I know. But that night when you sat outside waiting on me when Bran and Candice was here why didn't you leave when you realized I wasn't home? Why did you stay?" I asked him.

"I was at River Days when you and yo girls got into that fight with Dora and her cousins. It was so crazy and wild that by the time I made it to where y'all was y'all was being escorted out by security. Then I ran into Tim and his girl. We talked for a few minutes then I ran out to Hart Plaza, but y'all was being put into police cars. I came over here at like three thinking you was at home. When I realized you wasn't I just sat out there and waited on you." He said.

"Me and my girls didn't get out until like four something that morning they were trying to hold me on attempted murder because Dora was yelling she was pregnant." I said.

"I don't know why she told you I was her baby daddy, shit I can't be. I know I used a condom when I fucked her." Mike said as he laughed.

"She could have poked a hole in the condom like she's known for." I said, he looked at me then back at the road.

"She's one of those?" He asked me.

"One of what?" I asked him trying not to laugh.

"A trapper." He said.

"Yeah. She tried to trap the dude Gee who we both was messing with." I said.

"So, it was true huh?" He asked me as he got on the freeway.

"What was true? That we both messed with the same dude? Yeah I guess." I said as I looked out the window.

"How did that happen?" He asked me.

"How do you think it happened? Can we not talk about this?" I asked him.

"Ight, cool." He said.

When we got to Redford Brandy, Tim, Moe, and Candice were sitting outside of Tim's house.

"Well, glad you're finally out the bed." Candice said.

"Girl shut up. Y'all sold me out." I said as me and Mike walked up to them.

"Yo ass shouldn't have been spending your days in the bed."

"Whatever, what did you need to talk to me about?" I asked Tim.

"Tim knows who killed James, and he also knows who killed that girl Daivon." Candice said.

"Oh yeah, who?" I asked.

"Yo boy Gee and his homie Chris." Moe said. I burst out laughing.

"Y'all can't be serious. First off, why would Gee and Chris kill James? They didn't know him. And second off why would they kill Daivon, she was best friends with their girls." I said still laughing.

"You remember those licks I told you James said he hit?" Brandy asked me.

"Yeah, what about them?" I asked her.

"He hit those licks with me, and we hit Gee and Chris' spots. They found out and killed him." Tim said.

"How do you know this?" I asked.

"Come on na, for the right price the streets talk." Moe said.

"And how do y'all know Chris and Gee had something to do with Daivon's murder, and why do y'all even care?" I asked Brandy and Candice. But Tim answered.

"Daivon was black-mailing Gee. Gee and Chris fucked her one night while they were drunk. She and Gee did it two more times after that and she was going to tell Gee's girl on him. And Daivon was my woman." Tim said. I looked into his eyes; I could see that he wanted to cry.

"We gone get them hoe ass niggas." Mike said. I turned towards him and he was looking at me.

"And you're going to help us." Moe said to me.

"Why me?" I asked looking at all of them.

"Baby girl, you was fucking that nigga. I'm pretty sure you can get in touch with him and have him meet you somewhere." Tim said.

"And what if I can't and I won't do it?" I asked him.

"You're going to do it. And trust me you can. Wasn't y'all just texting the other day?" Tim asked me.

"How do you know I was texting him?" I asked him.

"Phone records." Mike said smiling.

"Y'all are out of y'all minds. I am not about to be a part of this." I said as I walked back towards my car.

"Can you at least do it for me and Brandon?" Brandy asked.

"Bran, I cannot help y'all set somebody up." I said.

"Why not? He killed the father of my child. He don't give a fuck about nobody but his self. Haven't you learned that yet? After all, you've been messing with him for some years and he still didn't give a fuck about yo feelings." Brandy said.

"Didn't you tell me and Bran you told him you was pregnant and he told you to get an abortion?" Candice asked. I didn't know what to do or say.

"Fine." I finally said before walking to my car.

Chris

Me, Gee, and Lil Chris were at Lil Chris' football practice. Gee and I were sitting on the sidelines when Lil Chris ran over to us.

"Daddy, did you see me catch that ball?" Lil Chris asked.

"Yeah, I saw you son. You did a good job." I said.

"Parian, didn't you play football?" He asked Gee.

"Yeah I did. And I was a wide receiver just like you." Gee said.

"Son you'd better get back out there." I said to my son.

"Okay." He said as he ran back over to his team.

"Man, this girl keep calling and texting my damn phone." Gee said as he looked at his phone.

"Who that?" I asked him.

"Jasmine. She texted me the day I went to the doctors with Leese. She told me about Daivon and that Daivon's dad was trying to get in touch with Leese." He said.

"What is he looking for Leese for?" I asked him.

“I don’t know. I’m not trying to tell her right now either. Her blood pressure already be sky high just thinking about that bitch.” He said.

“Man, just don’t tell her at all.” I said.

“I’m not. She don’t need to know. Fuck him and his daughter.” Gee said as I laughed.

“Parian, do you think my nanny is going to my game?” Lil Chris asked Gee.

“She said she was. And you know yo nanny don’t break her word.” Gee said as we reached my car.

“She’s coming, don’t worry son.” I said as my cell phone rang. It was Ashley.

“What?” I asked as I answered the phone.

“Where the fuck is my daughter? I haven’t seen her in almost two months!” She yelled, I knew she was either high, drunk or around her friends. But most likely it was all three of them.

“Ashley, stop all that damn yelling and that ain’t my problem. She's doing well without you.” I said.

“Chris, I want my fucking daughter.” She said.

“When you had her, you was bitching about me never having her so you could go club hopping. Remember that?” I said as I got in the car.

"I'm going to call the fucking police." She said.

"Go ahead, and then who's she going to stay with. They sure as hell ain't gone give her to yo unfit ass. Bitch you don't have a fucking job. You get food stamps and sell them so you can have money to get your hair and nails done. You didn't even feed my fucking daughter. I still give yo gold digging ass three hundred a month. But you not getting my daughter back. Plain and simple." I said hanging up the phone.

"What happened?" Gee asked me.

"That bitch Ashley talking about she calling the boys on me. She must have forgotten I'm paying her rent. And when my daughter was with her I was buying her clothes and shoes. She better go finish club hopping like she known to do." I was mad as hell.

"Let that shit go bro." Gee said as his phone rang. "This girl is getting on my last nerves. I need to change my fucking number." He said as he turned his phone off.

When we got to the house Katt was in the kitchen cooking dinner while Je'leese was in the dining room helping Christina with her homework.

"Hey daddy." Christina said as she got up from her seat and ran to hug me.

"Hey baby girl. You done with your homework?" I asked her.

"Yes. My nanny was just telling me about how she and mama Katt met you and my Parian." Christina said.

"That was the best day of my life. I met the woman I wanted to spend the rest of my life with." Gee said.

"Daddy, did you really sing to mama?" Christina asked me.

"Yes he did, him and your Parian was singing. They can sing too." Katt said as she walked into the dining room and stood next to me.

"Daddy, really? I want to hear you sing!" Christina said.

"I'll only sing if yo Parian sing with me." I said laughing.

"Come on man, I haven't sung a song in some years." Gee said as Katt sat down at the table.

"I want to hear y'all sing too." Lil Chris said.

"Chris, man let me talk to you away from them." Gee said. We walked into the living room close to the stairs.

"What's up?" I asked him smiling.

"If you want me to sing with you we gotta sing two songs, but not the full songs." Gee said smiling.

"What we singing?" He asked me.

"Where I Wanna Be and Did You Wrong. But I don't want to do the whole song to Where I Wanna Be. Just a lil verse then we can sing Did You Wrong." He said wanting to sing Pleasure P and Donnell Jones' songs.

"Ight man, you singing front and I'll sing back ground." I said laughing. We walked back to the dining room.

"Are y'all going to sing?" Katt asked us.

"Yeah, now hush woman." I said as everyone laughed. Je'leese was rubbing her stomach but she was looking at the paper in front of her. I knew no doubt these two songs were going to make her look at us. Well at Gee.

"I just left my baby girl a message saying I won't be coming home. I'd rather be alone. She doesn't fully understand me. That I'd rather leave then to cheat. If she give me some time, I can be the man she needs but there's a lot of lust inside of me and we've been together since our teenage years. I really don't mean to hurt her, but I need some time to be alone. But when you love someone you just don't treat them bad, oh how I feel so sad now that I want to leave, she's crying her heart to me how could you let this be. I just need some time to see, where I wanna be. Where I wanna be." We sung. Je'leese was looking at Gee with tears in her eyes and Katt was looking at me with a smile on her face.

"I don't want to lose this relationship so we gotta stay strong, don't wanna move on. I know you sick and tired of the fussing and the fighting and the cussing. But I love you, and you love me too. I did you wrong you did me wrong. I take you back, you take me back. I did you wrong girl, you did me wrong girl. I'll take you back, I'll take you back. No matter what you do. No matter what you say. No matter how far you go. Don't take your love away. Because I love you, and girl I want you, and girl I need you. So baby let's just work it out." We finished. By this time the tears were falling from Je'leese eyes and Katt had some in her eyes. I looked at Gee who was looking at Je'leese he had tears in his eyes too.

"Parian, what are you crying for?" Lil Chris asked.

"I think your mommy might have been cutting onions." Gee said as he smiled.

"That was nice." Katharine said as she rubbed Je'leese back.

"Y'all can sing I like y'all better than Barney." Christina said which made everyone laugh.

Je'leese

Everyone was getting ready for Lil Chris' game where he would be playing football. I was sitting on the sofa in the living room waiting on every one to finish getting dressed.

"You ready nanny?" Lil Chris asked me as he, Christina, Gee, Katt and Chris came down the stairs.

"Yeah I been ready. I've been waiting on y'all slow people." I said as I got up from the sofa. I was four and a half months pregnant and it was getting harder and harder for me to get up.

When we got to Piedmont Park on Park Dr., I sat in the car for a few minutes because my back was killing me.

"Are you okay?" Giovanni asked me.

"Yeah, I'm just having back pains." I said as I got out the car and walked with him over to where we had chairs set up to watch the games.

"What took you so long?" Katt asked me as I sat down between her and Giovanni. Chris was sitting next to Katt with Christina sleep in his arms.

"I was having back pains." I said as I took a sip of the water I had.

“Are you okay?” She asked me.

“Yeah.” I said as my cell phone rang. I pulled it out my pocket not recognizing the number.

“Hello.” I said.

“Is this Je’leese?” A female voice asked me.

“Yes this is, who is this?” I asked.

“This is Jasmine, are you around Gee?” Jasmine asked me I looked over at Giovanni who was watching the game. I got up from my chair and walked away from Giovanni, Katt, and Chris.

“No I’m not. Why?” I asked.

“I’ve been trying to get in touch with him for the longest.” She said.

“Giovanni has a family. He doesn’t have the time to talk to you.” I snapped.

“Je’leese, it’s nothing like that. Can you just pass a message along to him?” She asked me.

“Sure.” I said.

“A dude named Tim is looking for him and Chris. He thinks Chris and Gee killed this nigga named James and he also thinks Gee had something to do with Daivon been killed. Tim wants me to set Gee and Chris up, but that's something I can't do. I just want to warn him." Jasmine said.

"Thanks Jasmine, I'll make sure he gets the message." I said.

"Your welcome." She said as we hung up the phone. I walked back over to where they were sitting and Giovanni looked at me. I was debating on whether I should tell him or just keep it to myself. Then I thought about these twins I was carrying. They needed their father.

"We need talk away from everybody." I said.

"Who?" Katt asked.

"All four of us." I said.

"What am I going to do with Stina?" Chris asked.

"She's sleep she's not going to hear what we're saying." I said. They all got up and walked with me away from all the other parents and supporters of the game.

"What's up?" Katt asked me.

"Do y'all know a nigga named James?" I asked Chris and Giovanni. They looked at each other then back at me letting me know they knew who he was.

"We knew him, what about him though?" Giovanni asked.

“Jasmine just called me.” I said.

“What the fuck?” Chris asked.

“What the hell she called you for?” Katt asked.

“She said that she was trying to warn Giovanni since he wasn’t answering his phone for her.” I said looking at him.

“Yeah, I don’t have shit to say to her. But warn me about what?” He asked me.

“Y’all remember Daivon’s boyfriend Tim? Well I guess he knew the dude James or whatever. But Tim thinks y’all had something to do with James’ and Daivon’s death. And he’s trying to use Jasmine to get to y’all.” I said.

“Tim must be the one that’s been working with James.” Chris said.

“He probably was. But since that nigga looking for me, I’m going to him.” Giovanni said.

“Bro, you know I’m not gone let you go up there by yourself.” Chris said.

“I don’t think neither one of y’all are going.” Katt said.

“Why not? I’d rather go up there then have that nigga come down here.” Giovanni said.

"Giovanni, do you hear yourself talking? You have a fucking family now. You have two kids who are going to need you. If something was to happen to you what would your kids do? What would I do?" I asked him.

"Leesy, I'm doing this for you and my kids. I don't want that nigga to come down here and try something stupid like fucking with you." He said as he walked closer to me.

"Giovanni, I don't want you to go." I said as tears formed in my eyes.

"I don't want to go. But it's something I need to do. Don't worry Chris will have my back." He said.

"Who said Chris ass was going up there?" Katt asked as she folded her arms.

"Come on bae, you know I'm not gone let my nigga go up there by his self." Chris said.

"Well if both of y'all are going, then me and the kids are coming with you." Katt said.

"And if Katt go, then I'm going too." I said.

"No, fuck no!" Giovanni said.

Katherine

It was settled all of us were going back to Detroit, Michigan. Chris and Giovanni waited until the end of September to go because of the kids' school schedules. They thought about driving but with Je'leese about to be six months pregnant with twins they decided we needed to fly.

The day of the trip finally came. It was three in the morning, our plane didn't leave until five but we wanted to get up early so we could take a shower, eat breakfast, and put the bags in the car. Chris was sitting on the end of our bed with his back to me.

"Baby, what's wrong?" I asked him as I crawled to the foot of the bed.

"I don't want you or my kids up there." He said.

"Baby, everything is going to be fine. No one knows we left town, so they won't be expecting us to be at an airport. Your mother and father will be there to pick us up and bring us to your house. No one knows where you live so stop worrying." I said as I kissed him.

"I know everything is going to be fine. I still don't want y'all up there." He said.

"Baby, the kids miss Charles and Renee, and Christina needs to see her mother." I said.

"I know. But are you sure about meeting up with her?" He asked me.

"Yes I'm sure. As long as the bitch don't be on any stupid shit everything will be cool." I said smiling. After we ate breakfast, showered, and dressed we headed to the airport.

"Nanny, your stomach is big." Lil Chris said as we boarded the plane.

"Shhh, don't tell anyone else that." Je'leese said as we all laughed.

"I can't wait until my god brother gets here. We're going to take over the house." Lil Chris said.

"Oh really now? What about your parian and pops?" Chris asked him.

"All four of us can take over together. We're going to have four ladies to boss around." Lil Chris said as we all laughed.

"That's right." Gee said.

"Who are you going to be bossing around?" Je'leese asked Gee.

"Nobody boo." Gee said as they laughed. I was glad Je'leese and Gee were getting their old relationship back. They needed it, especially with two kids on the way.

When we touched down in Detroit I was so happy to be off that damn plane. My legs were killing me and I had a headache.

“Look, there’s granny and papa right there.” Lil Chris said as he pointed to Charles and Renee. We all walked over to them.

“Hey babies.” Renee said as Lil Chris and Christina hugged her.

“Hey Granny, we miss you and papa.” Lil Chris said.

“And we missed y’all more.” Renee said as she hugged me.

“God Leese, you’re big honey.” Renee said as she hugged Je’leese.

“I feel big.” Je’leese said smiling.

“I’m so happy for y’all. Is everything okay between y’all?” She asked Je’leese and Gee.

“Yes, everything is okay.” Gee said as he hugged Renee and shook Charles hand.

“I’m glad y’all could come back to visit us.” Charles said as he helped Gee and Christopher with the bags.

"We're going to keep the kids until y'all get settled at the house." Renee said.

"Ma, we're not staying here for long. The kids have to get back to school." Chris said.

"Then let me enjoy this time with my grandchildren." Renee said as we all laughed.

*****

"We'll be back." Chris said to me and Je'leese as we sat in the living room at our house.

"Where the hell are y'all going?" Je'leese asked.

"We got some business to handle." Gee said.

"Don't get into any trouble." I said.

"We're not." Chris said as he kissed me.

"I got a bad feeling about this trip." Je'leese said as they walked out the door.

"That makes two of us." I said.

"I hope everything be okay." She said.

"The boys are going to be okay. They know what they're doing." I said.

"I know, but I wish I didn't have this feeling and that it would go away." She said.

Jasmine

I was in the car on my way to meet Brandy and Candice at Sweetwaters when my cell phone rang. I didn't recognize the number and started not to answer it. But I did anyway.

"Hello." I said.

"Yo, where you at?" I heard Gee say from the other end of the phone.

"Driving down Jefferson. Why?" I asked him.

"Where are you headed to?" He asked me, I hated when he asked me a question without answering the question I asked him.

"I'm meeting Brandy and Candice there." I said.

"Well call me as soon as you leave them." He said.

"Okay." I said hanging up the phone. When I got to Sweetwaters Brandy and Candice were there but they weren't alone Moe, Mike, and Tim were there with them.

"What's up?" I asked sitting at the booth they were sitting at.

"Have you talked to your boy?" Mike asked me.

"No I haven't. And I told you once before when he calls me or answer my calls I'll be sure to let y'all know." I said. I was really irritated with Brandy and Candice; them bitches were really getting on my nerves. "Is this the reason y'all called me down here? To see if I've heard from Gee? Y'all could have asked me this shit over the phone." I said getting up from the booth and walking towards the door.

"Jas, wait!" Brandy called. I turned around and she and Candice were walking behind me.

"What?" I asked as I turned around.

"What the hell is wrong with you?" Brandy asked me.

"No, what the hell is wrong with you? Do it look like I wanted to get out my damn bed just so I could answer questions about Gee's ass?" I asked her.

"Tim wanted me to call and ask you that." Brandy said.

"Bran don't lie. You wanted to know if she talked to that nigga. We want him dead. And he's going to die." Candice said with venom in her eyes and voice. Brandy didn't have the same look in her eyes.

"Look, I gotta go. I told y'all if and when he calls me I'll let y'all know." I said as I walked off. I needed to talk to my cousin without Candice around.

"I'll call you once we leave from here." Brandy said.

"Okay." I said as I walked towards my car. But before reached it I heard Mike call my name, I turned around to face him.

"What do you want Mike?" I asked him.

"Why do you have an attitude with me? I didn't do you anything." He said.

"Because yo ass was using me this whole time. If you wanted to get at Gee why didn't you just say that in first place instead of playing with my feelings yet again?" I asked him

"Yo Jas, that was not my intentions. I didn't even know Gee was the nigga you was fucking with until that nigga Tim told me about it." He said.

"Am I supposed to believe that?" I asked him.

"I mean you can believe what you wanna believe. But I really didn't know. And I also meant what I said about me loving you." He said.

"Why do I need to help y'all get them? I don't want anything to do with that nigga. He made me get an abortion." I lied, I just didn't want anything to happen to Gee, but I wasn't going to tell Mike that.

"That should be reason enough. But Jas just do this for me!" Mike said.

"For fucking what? Just leave me out this shit." I said.

"Jasmine, you're already in it. All you need to do is keep calling and texting, trying to get his attention. And we you got it tell him to meet you somewhere, and Tim and Moe will handle the rest." He said.

"And what about me? What will happen when the police check his phone records and see how much I've been calling and texting him?" I asked him.

"If they come at you with some bullshit say that you were calling him because you was mad at him for making you get an abortion. You're going to be with me at the movies whenever you get in touch with him." Mike said.

"Y'all have this all figured out huh?" I asked him.

"Yeah, we owe this to James to get these niggas back, and make them pay." Mike said.

"Whatever." I said as I started walking back to my car.

"Can I see you later?" He asked me.

"Why later? Why not now?" I asked him.

"Come on Jas. I got some shit to handle." He said.

"But you're about to go back in there with my cousin, her sister-in-law, and yo two niggas. Oh okay." I said as I unlocked my car door and got in it. Mike was saying some shit, but I really didn't care to hear it at this point. I turned my car on and pulled out the parking lot. As soon as I got back on Jefferson I pulled my phone out and dialed the number Gee called me from earlier.

"Hello." He said.

"What's up? I just left Sweetwaters."

"Can you meet me in Flat Rock?" He asked me.

"At your house? Okay, I'll be there in like twenty." I said.

"Ight, good looking." He said before he hung up the phone. I knew it was gone take me longer to get to his house because I was going to my house so I could hop in the shower again.

When I got out the shower I had two missed calls from Gee, I called him back as I got in my car.

"Where you at?" He asked as soon as he picked up the phone.

"I'm sorry, my cousin and that nigga Tim went to my house. But I'm about to be getting off the freeway now." I told him.

"Aight, and yo ass better not be trying to set me up." He said, for a quick second I almost snapped on him.

"Gee, if I wanted to set you up I would have instead of calling yo girl and letting her know the plan." I said.

"Fasho shorty. Call me when you pulling up." He said.

"Okay." I said hanging up the phone. The nerve of that nigga to say I'd be trying to set him up.

Giovanni

"You sure this bitch ain't tryna set us up?" Chris asked me as he paced back in forth my living room floor.

"Chill man. She don't even know you over here. And naw, you know I can tell when somebody is lying to me. Shorty was straight forward with her shit." I said as I looked out the window again.

"Man, Ashley ass is blowing up my phone. I'm just about to tell Katt to go ahead and meet her ass at Fairlane." Chris said.

"You sure about that?" I asked him.

"Man, right now I'm not sure about nothing." He said as he laughed.

"Just wait until we're done handling this. You know Leesy isn't going to let Katt go by herself. And all it takes is for Ashley to say one thing out the way and Leesy gone hop on tip. And we don't need that." I said as my cell phone rang.

"Yo?" I said.

"I'm pulling up." Jasmine said as I looked out the window.

"Aight, come in." I said.

"Yo girl in there? I don't got time to deal with her today." She said.

"Nah, she not here and she not gone be here." I said.

"Okay." She said. I looked out the window until Jasmine knocked on the door. Chris answered the door.

"What's up?" Chris asked her.

"Hey." She said as she walked past Chris.

"How you doing?" I asked her.

"I'm doing good, just ready for all this shit to be over with." She said.

"Why?" I asked her as Chris looked at me.

"They're tracking yo phone records. They see you texting other people back, and answering and calling other people but you're not texting and answering my calls, nor is you calling me back. That shit is irk-some." She said as she sat down on my sofa.

"So, how did all this shit come about?" Chris asked her.

"I went out too Redford one day with this nigga Mike I was fucking with and I met these dudes named Tim and Moe. After that Moe and Tim been hanging with my cousin who is James' baby mama and her sister-in-law who is James' sister. One day Mike called me and said Tim wanted to talk to me. We went to Redford and Tim told me, my cousin, and her sister-in-law that he knew who killed James and Daivon. I asked him who and he told me y'all did it. I laughed and asked him why would y'all want to kill them two? He told me him and James was the ones that hit y'all spots and he also said that he knew Daivon was black-mailing you and wanting to tell yo girl about what y'all been doing." She said.

"Damn, so what's your part in all this?" I asked her.

"They want me to call you and tell you to meet me somewhere. But I'm not going to be waiting on you. Moe and Tim are. I'll be at the movies with Mike." She said.

"What does yo cousin and her sister got to do with this?" Chris asked her.

"I don't know. I haven't been hanging around them because they be with Tim and Moe so much. But I don't think my cousin wants anything to do with this. But James' sister wants revenge for her brother." She said.

"Look, we didn't have anything to do with that nigga James being killed and we didn't have shit to do with Daivon being killed. I wasn't even in town when that bitch got killed." I said.

“Where was you at?” She asked me like I knew she was.

“I was in Cali with Chris, Katt, Je’leese and my god children.” I lied.

“Well, whatever you do watch your back because I’m pretty sure the plan isn’t going to go thru if they see you riding around somewhere.” She said.

“Good looking on that info. I’ll call you later to check up on you.” I said as she stood up. I gave her a hug and she walked to the door.

“It was good to see you again, I miss you.” She said.

“It was good to see you too. And I miss you too.” I lied, I really didn’t miss her. But I’ll tell her whatever she wants to hear just to get what I wanted.

After Jasmine left Chris and I headed over to his house in Oak Park so we could take Christina to see her mama.

“I want to go with y’all.” Katt said.

“Baby, why can’t you just stay here?” Chris asked her.

“Chris, do it look like I want you to go around that bitch?” She asked.

"Baby, I'm not going to fuck her. I'm just taking my daughter to see her." Chris said.

"Oh, I know you're not going to fuck her because I'm going with you." Katt yelled.

"And if Katt go then I'm going too." Je'leese said.

"Leese, you pregnant, you need to stay here." I said.

"Giovanni, I am not staying here. We might as well load the car up and get to going." Je'leese said as Katt laughed.

"Man, y'all so damn crazy." Chris said as he walked out the door. I helped Je'leese off the sofa and she walked out the door behind Katherine. I locked the house up then went to get in the car.

"Where are we meeting this bitch anyway?" Katt asked.

"Her house." Chris said.

"Hell no, tell that bitch to meet you in Fairlane parking lot." Katt said from the back seat as I got in the passenger seat.

"Are you serious Katherine?" Chris asked her.

"Yes I'm serious Christopher." Katt said. I just laughed and put on my seat belt. We had to go to Chris' parents' house to get Christina. We left Lil Chris there and headed to Fairlane.

When we got to Fairlane Christina was in the backseat sleep on Je'leese's stomach.

"My babies don't like Stina being on me." Je'leese said laughing.

"They don't like when nobody touch yo ass." Katt said.

"They like when daddy touching her." I said laughing. I turned around and looked at Je'leese, she was blushing. I was happy that we were back to being how we use to be, or somewhat like it. Je'leese still told me that she didn't trust me and she didn't know if she could ever trust me again. But I was going to do everything in my power to gain her trust back. I did little small things for her, I even bought her things whenever I want to the mall. I knew that buying her things wasn't going to make her trust me but I still did it.

"Katt, can you wake Stina up?" Chris asked as he looked down on his phone.

"Stina, wake up." Katherine said.

"Nigga, it's about muthafucking time you brought me my fucking daughter!" Ashley yelled as she walked over to the car.

"Ashley, don't bring yo rat ass over here with that fucking yelling." Chris said.

"Fuck you, where the fuck is my daughter?" Ashley asked.

"She's in the back seat." Chris said as he got out the car. He walked around to Katt's side with Ashley following him.

"Nigga, I know you don't got this bitch holding my fucking daughter." Ashley said once the back door was opened.

"Watch yo mouth man." Chris said.

"Fuck that, I'm taking my fucking daughter with me. I don't give a damn what you say. My fucking daughter coming home with me." Ashley said.

"I want to stay with my daddy and mama Katt." Christina cried as she realized what her mama said.

"Christina, stop all that damn whining and get yo ass out the car." Ashley said.

"Ashley, stop fucking cussing around my daughter." Chris said in a low voice.

"Nigga, fuck you!" Ashley yelled at Chris. "Bitch, let my daughter go so she can get out the car." She added to Katt. I got out the car because I knew it was going to be some bullshit. Katt put Christina down on the seat and got out the car. Christina moved closer to Je'leese and was nearly on her lap.

"Ashley, I don't know you, and you damn sure don't know me. But you will not disrespect me and you will not make that little girl go somewhere she don't want to go." Katt said.

"Bitch, who the fuck is you to tell me what I can do with my fucking daughter? Have you lost your mind? My daughter is not yo fucking child. You worry about yo bitch ass son." Ashley said before Katt hit her in her mouth.

"Bitch, speak on my son again and I'm gone beat the breaks off yo rat ass." Katt said. Ashley tried to hit Katherine but Chris grabbed her hand. By this time Je'leese was out the car. I went stood next to her making sure she didn't get hit nor did she hit anybody. I didn't need her out there fighting or trying to fight.

"I tried to be civilized with yo ass, but you don't want that. Na get the fuck on. Yo ass can't see my daughter no fucking more. Call the police, call whoever you want because they'll give her to me before they let her back with yo rat ass." Chris said as he pushed Ashley back, she fell on the ground.

"Bitch!" Katt yelled as she kicked her in her face.

“Come on baby.” I said to Je’leese as I helped her back in the car.

Chris

I was really pissed as hell at that shit that Ashley pulled and especially when she spoke on my son. I really wanted to punch her ass in her mouth, but I held myself together. The kids were spending all their time with my mom and pops before we headed back to Atlanta after we handled our business. Gee and Leesy had been spending the night at my house just in case Tim and his niggas tried to run up in Gee's house while he was sleep. We didn't fully trust Jasmine and the shit she was saying so we kept our options open about what we were going do. Katherine and Je'leese tried to get info on the plans, but we didn't tell them anything. And we didn't plan on telling them anything.

"Chris, get up." Katt said as she shook me.

"I am woke. What's up?" I said sitting up. It was pitch dark in the room but I could still see Katt, she had a worried expression on her face.

"What do you and Gee have planned?" She asked me. I couldn't believe she would have woken me up just to ask me that. I was so glad that I wasn't really asleep.

"Katt, you woke me up to ask me that?" I asked her pretending I was.

"I know you weren't sleep Christopher." She said.

"How do you know that?" I asked her.

"How long have we been sleeping in the same bed?" She asked me.

"Don't think you know me." I said smiling.

"I do know you, and don't think I don't know that you're trying to change the damn subject." She said.

"Come on baby. When have I ever told you something about what I do in the streets?" I asked her.

"You haven't." She said.

"And that's not going to change for nothing." I said as I pulled her closer to me.

"Baby, I'm just worried about you." She said.

"There's no need to be worried. I'm going to be fine. Me and Gee are going to handle our business, then when we're done we're getting on the first plane out of this thing." I said as I kissed her.

"Okay Chris, but promise me you won't end up in jail or worse. You or Gee because I don't know what Leese would do if she lose him." She said.

"Baby, I promise you, me or Gee will not end up in jail or dead." I said.

The next morning, Katherine and Leese were sitting in the kitchen eating breakfast.

"Y'all didn't think about me or Gee?" I asked them.

"Y'all plates are in the oven." Katherine said as she placed a spoonful of eggs in her mouth. I walked over to the oven just as Gee walked into the kitchen.

"What y'all eating?" Gee asked.

"What does it look like we're eating?" Je'leese asked him.

"I don't know, that's why I asked."

"We're eating some Coney Island. Didn't nobody feel like cooking." Katt said.

"So what are y'all plans for the day?" Je'leese asked as I sat down at the table with my plate.

"Um, we got some business to handle. We're trying to be outta here by tomorrow morning." Gee said.

"I can't wait until we get back. I miss my Sleep Number bed." Je'leese said as she smiled.

Jasmine

I just got off the phone with Mike confirming our movie date. Gee called me before I got on the phone with Mike and told me to meet him in Southwest where he will be. I told Mike and Mike was suppose to pass the message along to Tim. I was getting off my bed when my cell phone rang. It was Brandy.

“Hello.” I said.

“Where are you at?” She asked me.

“The house, about to get ready to meet Mike, where are you at?” I asked her.

“About to be pulling up in front of your building.” She said.

“Okay, is Candice with you?” I asked her.

“No, she’s with Tim.” She said sounding bitter.

“Well just come in, the door will be open.” I said as I got up and went and unlocked the door.

“Okay.” She said as we hung up the phone.

“Look at you.” Brandy said as she walked into my room where I was curling my hair.

“No, look at you, you look good.” I said.

"Why thank you, you know I tries." She said as she turned around so I could see her.

"Who did your hair?" I asked her.

"That girl NeNe that live in Southwest." She said.

"Well, she need to hook me up." I said as I looked at my hair.

"Girl, and she cheap with it." Brandy said.

"Well the next time I need my hair done she's who I'm calling." I said.

"Is everything set for tonight?" She asked me.

"Yeah, are you going to be there?" I asked her.

"Yeah, but I don't want to be there." She said.

"Then don't go. You can stay over here and I won't tell anyone that you're over here." I said trying to keep my cousin safe.

"I don't know. That nigga Tim is crazy as hell. He's already beating on Candice." She said shaking her head and sitting on my bed.

"Where's Cathy, didn't you tell me she was talking about moving in with him?" I asked her.

"Cathy's with her, she did move out of her parent's house. Her mama said she wasn't going to live to see a New Year because when she went over there she had bruises on her face." Brandy said.

"I know James probably turning over in his grave." I said as I turned around to look at her.

"Hell yeah. You know Candice is his favorite and youngest sister." She said.

"She need to leave him alone before he started hitting Cathy." I said.

"She won't listen to anybody. She thinks she's in love already. But that nigga is in love with a dead woman." She said.

We talked until Mike called me and told me he was outside.

"Are you going to stay here?" I asked her.

"Yeah." She said as she walked out my room and I followed her, she walked into the guest room and I walked out the front door.

"You look good." Mike said as he got out the car and opened the door for me.

"Thank you." I said smiling. "What movie theater are we going to?" I asked him.

"Fairlane, just in case something goes wrong in Southwest and I need to get there in a hurry," he said. I didn't say anything; I just buckled my seat beat and looked out the window.

Chris

"Is everything ready?" Gee asked some lil niggas that use to work at our shops.

"Yeah, it's just suppose to be two niggas right?" The one named Josh said.

"Yeah, and if it's three we can handle them niggas." I said.

"We already know that." The one named Ant said. We were sitting in an abandon house on Electric.

"What times these niggas suppose to be coming?" I asked Gee.

"She said she told them at eight forty because her movie started at eight fifty." Gee said, I looked down at my watch it was eight thirty three.

"Man, if that bitch Jasmine set us up she gotta go." I said.

"She already gotta go regardless. We don't keep no witnesses." Gee said.

The plan was for Jasmine to tell the dudes that Gee would be upstairs in the house waiting on her so they could fuck. They're not expecting me or no other niggas to be here. The outside of the house looked abandon, but because most of the houses out here looked like that they would think the inside was fully furnished.

"Yo, they here." Gee said. He was looking out the window.

"Get in y'all places." I said getting behind the door. As soon as they came into the building I was gone come from behind the door with my guns pointed at their heads. The only light came from the one in the bathroom and the one upstairs. It took like ten minutes for them niggas to walk up the sidewalk and into the house. They opened the door not even checking behind them. Gee was sitting on the sofa with his phone out.

"Got yo bitch ass now." Tim said.

"You think you got me?" Gee asked looking at them smiling.

"Bitch ass niggas put y'all fucking head down." I said as I walked from behind them.

"Man, fuck! That bitch set us up." The other who I'm guessing was Moe said. Ant and Josh walked from out the kitchen pointing their guns towards them.

"What y'all bitches gone do? Y'all gone put y'all heat down or are we going to have a shoot out?" Gee asked, they slowly but surely put their guns down.

"Now, tell me the reason y'all niggas wanted to steal from me and my mans?" I asked as I walked around in front of them.

“Man niggas wasn’t eating! Y’all niggas was eating good.” Moe said.

“We didn’t think y’all would mind us taking some off y’all plates.” Tim said.

“Niggas, that’s where your wrong! We got family that need to eat. We didn’t have time to feed no other niggas besides the one that starved with us.” Gee said.

“Fuck y’all niggas and the niggas y’all was eating with.” Moe said.

“Oh yeah nigga?” Josh asked. He looked at Gee then at me, we both nodded our heads giving him a signal to go. He opened fire with an AK and lit Moe’s ass up.

“That’s what I’m talking about.” Ant said.

“Man, y’all couldn’t have thought I was gone let shit slide did y’all? Y’all killed my right hand mans, then turned around and killed my lady? I love that girl with everything in me.” Tim said as me, Gee, Ant, and Josh gave each other signals.

“Well nigga, didn’t ya mama ever tell yo punk ass not to love these hoes?” Gee asked as we opened fire on his ass.

“Man that shit sounded like a fucking firework show.” Josh said as we were back in my car.

"Gee, call that bitch Jasmine and tell her to meet you so we can get this shit over with." I said, I was ready to get home to my lady.

Jasmine

I was watching Kevin Hart's move 'Let Me Explain' with Mike when my cell phone vibrated, I looked at it and it was a text message from an unknown number.

"I need you in that nigga Mike to meet us at Brandy's baby's daddy's people's house." The number said.

"Who is this?" I texted back.

"Tim, tell yo cousin Brandy and home girl Candice to meet us too." Tim said. I looked at Mike then showed him the message, he nodded his head took a sip of his drink then stood up and walked past me. I sat there for a few more seconds then got up and followed him.

"Are you sure we should be meeting them?" I asked Mike as we walked out the movies.

"Yeah ma, everything cool. Call your girls and let them know what he said." He said as he grabbed my hand aand we walked to his car. I called Brandy and Candice and they both told me they would meet me there. Candice was going to get there first because she was downtown.

When we got off the freeway on Schaefer I had this weird feeling in my stomach.

"Something just don't feel right." I said.

“What do you mean?” Mike asked me as he stopped at the red light.

“I don’t know. I just have a weird feeling in my stomach.” I said.

“Is it a baby?” Mike asked me smiling.

“Didn’t you use a condom?” I asked him.

“Hell yeah, but if you was pregnant it could be by that nigga Gee.” He said. I wanted to smack the hell out of him.

“Nigga, Gee and I never fucked without a condom, matter of fact I’ve never fucked a nigga without a condom.” I said as I rolled my eyes at him.

“I didn’t mean it like that ma.” He said.

“Yeah whatever.” I said as he turned down Bassett.

“What the hell is going on?” He asked me as we pulled in front of the house. Brandy was on the ground leaning over something. At first I thought it was Brandon but when I got out the car I saw it was Candice.

“What happened?” I asked her.

“I don’t know, when I pulled up she was already on the ground.

“Did you call the police?” Mike asked her.

“Yeah.” She said as she stood up. “She’s dead, I can’t find a pulse.” She said as she looked at her sister-in-law again.

The next thing I heard was “BOOM!” “BOOM!” Two shots that sounded like they came from a shot gun, I dropped to the ground for like two minutes before I made sure whoever was shooting wasn’t going to shoot again. I stood up and saw Brandy and Mike had a bullet in their heads. Tears instantly fell down my face. I looked at them one more time before I hopped in Mike’s car and got the fuck on before the police showed up.

Katherine

“I’m going too get in the shower maybe that will stop this damn pain.” Je’leese said as she got up from the sofa and walked up the stairs.

“Okay.” I said. We were watching Halloween. I was so into the movie that when my cell phone rang I jumped. And the movie wasn’t even that scary. It was from and unknown caller, I answered it.

“Hello.” I said.

“Baby, it’s me. Have everything packed up. Me and Gee about to roll through and get you and Leese, help her put Gee things away too.” Chris said. I had a sigh of relief knowing that they were okay.

"Okay." I said.

"I love you." He said.

"I love you more." I said as we hung up the phone.

"Leese!" I called out as I walked up the stairs.

"Huh?" She asked me, I walked into one of the guest bedrooms and stood in the door way.

"Gee and Chris are on their way to get us. They said for us to have our things packed up." I said.

"Okay." She said. I walked out the room and into me and Chris' room.

As soon as I was done packing my clothes I put Christopher's few clothes in the suit case and rolled them by the door.

"KATT!!" Je'leese yelled. I dropped the bags as I ran into the room.

"What?" I asked her, she was standing in the middle of the floor with her robe wrapped around her body.

"I think my water just broke." She said holding the bottom of her stomach, I looked at the floor and sure enough there was fluid on the floor.

"Damn. Put some clothes on, I'm about to call Gee and Chris and get the car ready, or would you rather for the ambulance to come?" I asked her.

"I don't care!" She yelled. I ran out the room and back into my room, I grabbed my phone and dialed 911.

"911 what is your emergency?" The dispatcher asked me.

"We need an ambulance!" I said as I walked back into the room with Je'leese.

"What's the problem?" The dispatcher asked me as Je'leese yelled out.

"My sister is six months pregnant and is going into labor." I said as I helped Je'leese with her shirt.

"What's the address?" The dispatcher asked me. I gave her the address and she told me that an ambulance was three minutes away.

Giovanni

Me and Chris just dropped Josh and Ant off at their cribs, then we headed to Chris' house.

"Man, I can't believe you let that bitch live!" Chris said.

"She didn't deserve to die. She did help us." I said.

"What happens if that bitch go to the cops?" He asked me.

"Man, I don't think she's gonna do that, besides that bitch is an accessory to that nigga Tim and that other nigga murder." I said really hoping my decision of letting Jasmine stay alive didn't come back to bite me in the ass. I was about to say something when my phone rang. I looked at the screen and it was Katt.

"Hello." I said.

"Je'leese is in labor." She said out of breath.

"It's too early, what hospital are y'all at?" I asked her.

"We're at Henry Ford on Grand Blvd." She said.

"Ight, we'll be there soon." I said.

"Please hurry up. She's crying about you not being here." She said.

"Ight." I said hanging up the phone.

"What happened?" Chris asked me as soon as I hung up the phone.

"Man, Leesy went into labor, she's at Henry Ford, we need to hurry up and get there." I said.

“We’re like fifteen minutes away.” Chris said as he looked at me.

When we got too the hospital we parked the car in a Handicap spot and I called Katt.

“Third floor room three thirteen.” Katt said. I ran into the hospital, and Chris followed me. We had security following behind us because we wouldn’t stop running.

“Gentlemen, what are you running for?” The security guard asked.

“My wife is in labor and I’m trying to make it in time.” I said as the elevator doors opened.

“Please slow down when y’all get up there.” The security guard said as the doors closed on her. I was so glad when they opened again, I ran until I was standing in front of Je’leese’s room.

“Ahhhh, it hurts! Please get these babies out of me!” Je’leese yelled as soon as I opened the door.

“Look Leese, Gee’s here.” Katt said as she moved out the way and let me get next too the bed.

“Where have you been Giovanni?” Je’leese asked me with sweat on her forehead in her eyes.

“I was at Charles and Renee’s house.” I lied

“Well, it took yo ass long enough to get here.” She said.

It was around six in the morning when a doctor walked into the room. Je'leese was still in pain, Chris and Katt were sitting down on the chairs that were in the room. But I was standing up because Je'leese told me I had better not get comfortable while she was in so much pain.

"Are you ready to push Mrs. Smith?" Dr. Alaric asked.

"I've been ready to push since I got in here!" Je'leese said.

"Well, it's time to get these babies into this world." Dr. Alaric said as he and the nurse's positioned themselves.

At seven twenty seven a.m Je'leese gave birth to our son Giovanni Robert Smith Jr. weighing 6lbs 8oz and 10inches. And at seven thirty seven a.m she gave birth to our daughter Jiovanna Marie Smith weighing 5lbs, 6oz, and 9inches. They both were born on October 10th 2013.

"She's beautiful." I said as I held my daughter in my arms. Je'leese had Giovanni Jr. in her arms.

"Thank you." She said looking at me.

"For what?" I asked her.

"For giving me this handsome son and that beautiful daughter," she said, I reached over and kissed her forehead happy that my kids were born without any health problems even though they both were premature.

Je'leese

A week after I gave birth to my twins, all three of us were discharged from the hospital. Me, Katt, Jiovanna, and Giovanni Jr. were in the lobby waiting for Chris and Giovanni to pull the up to the front entrance. It was the fall and it was so windy outside that my kids had two blankets covering them up and I had on a jacket.

"Where is Lil Chris and Stina?" I asked Katt.

"Renee and Charles are bringing them over to the house now." Katt said as Giovanni and Chris walked back into the hospital. Katt rolled me outside in the wheel chair as Giovanni and Chris carried Giovanni Jr. and Jiovanna to the car.

"Man Gee, Jiovanna looks just like you." Chris said as we all got in the car.

"That's my baby girl, of course she looks just like me." Giovanni said laughing.

"Yeah, but Lil Gee don't look nothing like you." Chris said as we all laughed.

"That's because he looks more like his mommy than daddy." Giovanni said.

"So y'all got y'all a mommy's boy and a daddy's girl." Katt said as Chris pulled off.

"Yes we do." I said.

"They're both going to be spoiled rotten." Chris said.

"And get anything they want." Giovanni said.

"Little Miss. Jiovanna may look just like her daddy but she already has an attitude like her mean ass mommy. Don't want anybody holding her unless it's her daddy and sometimes her mommy." Katt said.

"She done created a monster." Chris said.

"My baby girl is not mean." Giovanni said as he looked at the twins.

"Who told you that damn lie?" Katt asked.

"Baby, is my little girl mean?" Gee asked me.

"Yes she is. She hardly let me hold her unless I'm feeding her. You know that." I said smiling.

"I feel bad for y'all when she gets older. She's going to be hell to deal with." Chris said.

"No she's not. She's going to be a good little spoiled daddy's girl." Giovanni said as we all laughed.

"She and Stina are going to drive Lil Chris and Lil Gee up the walls." Katt said.

"Why is that?" Chris asked as he got on the freeway.

"Because they're going to be some beautiful teenage girls. They're going to have a lot of little boys trying to get their attention." Katt said.

"My daughter is going to know at an early age not to talk to any boys until she's twenty one." Giovanni said.

"But Lil Chris and Lil Gee, they are going to have females chasing after them so crazy." Chris said.

"No the hell they're not." Me and Katt said at the same time.

"Chill out y'all. They're boys that's what supposed to happen." Giovanni said.

"My son will not have any females chasing after him. He's not going to have a girlfriend until he graduate high school." I said.

"Yeah whatever Leese." Giovanni said.

"When are we going back to Atl? I really do miss my bed." I said changing the subject.

"We can leave in two days. I got something to take care of." Giovanni said.

"And what is that?" I asked him.

"Don't worry about it." He said.

Chris pulled up in the parking lot of me and Giovanni's house and I was confused.

"What are we doing here? I thought we were going back to y'all place?" I asked Chris.

"We was, but Gee said he wanted to come over here for a while. He needs to add some things to his bags." Chris said. I looked at Gee and he was looking at Jiovanna who started crying.

"Aw man, the cry baby is waking up." Katt said as she turned around and laughed. Giovanni placed the pacifier in her mouth and she stopped crying for the time being.

"Gee let me and Katt take the babies inside while you help Leese out the car. I know she's probably still in pain." Chris said.

"Alright." Giovanni said as they all got out the car. Giovanni walked around the car and helped me out. Katt and Chris were getting the kids out the car. Once we got to the door we heard some footsteps behind us. We turned around and four police officers were standing there.

"Giovanni Smith and Christopher Butler y'all are under arrest for the murders off Daivon Hampton, Timothy Anderson, Brandy Wright, and Candice Anthony." One of the officers said.

"Man, can't this wait until I take my kids in the house?" Giovanni asked. I didn't know what to say or do at this point. I just started crying. Giovanni opened the door and Chris and Katt placed the babies on the table that was in the living room.

"Baby, everything is going to be okay." Giovanni said as he kissed me on my forehead, he kissed the twins then walked over to the officers.

"Baby, call the lawyers and tell them what we're being charged with. We didn't do shit so we should be home before sun down." Chris said to Katt as he kissed her on the lips.

"Please don't take him. I need him. My kids need him." I said as a second officer read them their rights and placed handcuffs on them.

"Leesy stop crying. Everything is going to be fine. Just take care of my kids. I'm going to be fine and I'll be home to y'all soon." Giovanni said as they walked him outside. My twins started crying as I walked with them. Katt was still standing where Chris left her on the phone with somebody; I was hoping it was their lawyer. I stood out in the driveway until the two police cars pulled off with Giovanni in one and Chris in the other one.

"The lawyer is on his way to the station now." Katt said as she picked Giovanni Jr up. I walked over to Jiovanna and picked her up. I sat down on the sofa still crying. I didn't know what I was going to do with out Giovanni. I needed him to be there for me and our kids. I knew it was a bad choice to come back up here.